bo🪲ger

Hey Arianne I hope you enjoy it!

BOOGER
a novel

WHY KNOT BOOKS
5443 Eighth Line,
Erin, ON, N0B 1T0
Canada

E-book: 978-0-9810609-6-5
Book: 978-0-9810609-5-8

519 833 1242
johnnydenison@hotmail.com

bo🫘ger

(a novel)

J O H N   D E N I S O N

WHY KNOT
BOOKS

Welcome to Shipstead, California

JW's real name is John Winston Lennon Martin. He's fifteen-years old and right now he's on his bike heading down Harper Ave. In Shipstead, California, when you say you're going *downtown* you mean it. Almost straight down. JW hasn't pushed his pedals since Grove St.

"Beam me up! Beam me up!" squawks Janis Joplin, the one-winged parrot.

"Approaching warp speed!" JW shouts back.

They're quite a sight flying along. JW hunched over the handlebars, his blond hair blowing in the wind, his bright orange t-shirt sticking out back like someone is pulling on it. Janis leaning forward, her toes wrapped around the hockey tape JW has added to his handlebars to help Janis hold on. Her bright green, yellow and red feathers puff and flatten with the breeze and if you knew her better you'd know she was smiling. She likes going to *The Pet Vet* with JW.

"Make my day!" Janis squawks.

JW just grins.

It's Saturday and as usual the Crummie Burger parking lot is full. JW ditches his bike in the rack and heads for the picnic table on the beach where his buddies from the basketball team, Miguel Sanchez and Ty Randall, are busy giving their orders to Niki Sanjay. Niki is in JW's math class. He doesn't know her at all, she's new in town, but she looks good in her shiny silver shorts and tight, silver Crummie's t-shirt.

The outdoor speakers crackle. Here comes the 6 p.m. drum roll followed by the *Bong of the Gong*. Inside Crummie's and out in the picnic area everyone gets to their feet and holds hands. JW joins the circle between Ty and Niki. The loudspeakers crackle again and the Crummie Burger theme song fills the air:

We hope you have a Crummie Day,
We hope you have a Crummie Day.
How we love to hear you say,
Oh Man, I've had a Crummie Day!

The idea is to sing the words as loudly as you can while at the same time doing the dip, turn and kick thing. It's stupid fun and the more you do it the more stupid fun it becomes especially with a one-winged parrot perched on your shoulder singing her heart out.

"I must have done that two hundred times and it still makes me laugh," JW says sitting down.

"Crummie day! Crummy Day!"

Niki smiles at JW. "Who's your friend?"

"You old hag," Janis says. Niki laughs.

"This is Janis Joplin, the one-winged wonder."

"I thought Janis Joplin was a singer?"

"She was. My dad names everything after old rock n'roll stars."

"He 'as a python named Gerry and the Pacemakers," Ty says.

"And a gorilla called Mick Jagger," adds Miguel.

"And he's named after John Lennon," Ty says pointing at JW.

Niki gives the boys a look that means *you don't expect me to believe any of this, do you?* She puts her hand out to stroke Janis' feathers.

"Your mother wears army boots! Your mother wears army boots!"

Niki's smile disappears. She looks at JW with hurt in her eyes. "What can I get you?"

"Cheeseburger, fries, chocolate shake. Please."

JW watches Niki turn away. She's upset. He can tell by the way she moves. What was that about?

"And are all the wee animals stuffed and happy, JW?" Ty asks in his thick Scottish accent. Ty's been living in California for two years but he's trying hard to keep his accent. The *wee lassies* like it.

JW's dad, Dr. Martin *he's so nice*, is one of two veterinarians in Shipstead. He owns *The Pet Vet* on Main Street and every other Saturday afternoon JW and Janis Joplin ride to the clinic where they check on the animals and feed them.

"I managed not to lose Hamlet this time," JW says. Hamlet is a Great Dane, the size of a small pony. He's boarding at *The Pet Vet* and last week the leash JW had been using to walk Hamlet had given up. It was one of those leashes that comes out of its plastic case when you push the button except this time it never stopped coming out and JW was an hour chasing Hamlet around Main Street. And he only caught him because Hamlet, The-Not-So-Great-Dane, as JW was calling him, finally stopped at Crummie's for a cheeseburger. Or four.

"Taking Hamlet for a walk is like being a water-skier," JW says. "I'm holding on but I'm definitely not steering the boat."

Miguel and Ty grin at this.

"What's going on?" JW looks over at the corner of the parking lot where the City-TV *On-the-Move Van* is set up with its huge television screen facing Crummie's.

"They're intervuuin' the famous Jack Granite." Ty imitates the famous Jack Granite neon smile. The one with the Dazzling White Teeth. The one that all Shipstead mothers use as the reason why it's so important to brush your teeth. *Don't you want to be a famous astronaut like Jack Granite? Think what you'll be if your teeth are yellow?*

Zoo keeper?

Jack Granite is the town's biggest celebrity. He used to be an astronaut but now he spends his time developing property around Shipstead. He even donated the land for the new high school in town, Granite High.

He's also not married, handsome and the richest man for miles.

The big screen flickers to life and with it comes 2001 space music. The boys watch as Eagle, the lunar module, lands on the moon for the first time.

"Houston, Tranquility Base here. The Eagle has landed."

"Roger, Tranquility. We copy you on the ground. You got a bunch of guys about to turn blue. We're breathing again. Thanks a lot."

That must have been cool, JW thinks, first man on the moon. JW'd like to be the first at something and he soon will be. He just doesn't know it yet.

"This year we're celebrating the 40th anniversary of Man landing on the moon. Forty years ago Neil Armstrong stepped out of Eagle, the Apollo 11 lunar module, and said these words heard around the world, 'That's one small step for a man, one giant leap for mankind.'"

Niki arrives with their orders and makes a point of not looking at JW. She must know Janis was just kidding, thinks JW. Who can figure out girls?

JW hands Janis a French fry.

"Better late than never!"

"Hi, I'm Linda White. Today, we're on location in Shipstead, California, with former astronaut, Jack Granite. Jack, I can't believe it's been forty years since Neil Armstrong first walked on the moon."

JW finds it weird seeing Jack Granite great big on the TV screen when he can also see him standing five feet away from the van in the parking lot.

"I think what's even more astounding, Linda, is that only 66 years passed between the Wright Brothers' first flight at Kitty Hawk and our landing on the moon. That is an incredible achievement."

Look out, here comes the famous Jack Granite neon smile again. The one with the Dazzling White Teeth. The boys groan.

"Get stuffed! Get stuffed!"

"I understand Jack you'll be flying to Cape Canaveral to be part of the big celebrations."

"That's right, Linda. There'll be a shuttle leaving for the international space station the day before the ceremony. Then a landing module will be sent from the station to land on the moon. Astronaut Denise Franklin will place another flag, this time of the United Nations, beside the original American Flag. It should be something."

"C'mon, you old hag," JW says standing up.

"What's the prize? What's the prize?"

"I'll give you a big kiss."

"Second prize, second prize!" squawks Janis hopping onto JW's outstretched arm. JW turns back to his friends.

"Has anybody heard what Dougie's doing for Inventors?"

Dougie (say it like you're yelling *DEE-FENCE* at the football game) is Douglas "Don't Call Me Dougie" Brown, JW's archrival in physics class. Unfortunately for JW, when the marks are handed out, JW's always the one in second place. And Inventors is like Science Fair only way cooler.

"I hear he's trying to invent a no-water toilet…"

"Good idea in California."

"…and I hear it's not going well."

"Even better," says JW.

JW looks back. Miguel and Ty are still on their bikes but they're both standing up doing that way to the left, way to the right thing that means they're within seconds of getting off their bikes and walking. JW is out of gas too. He hops off and waits for the others.

"Ach mun, I'll be glad when I can drive," Ty says. There's something about the hill always winning that gets to boys in Shipstead.

"When I go to my dad's there isn't a hill for miles." This is Miguel talking. "You can ride all day and not get tired."

The boys think about this.

"Remember Miguel," JW says, "when we had to write that poem about Shipstead in Mr. Mark's class? Couldn't be more than ten words."

"That's because he didn't want to spend more than two minutes marking them."

"Do you blame him?"

"Nope, so what did you write, JW?"

JW stops. Any reason to stop going uphill is grabbed at. JW clears his throat.

"In Shipstead it's hard going uphill,
But down's a thrill."

"You got that right," Miguel says. "Mine was:

Crummie's below, Granite's above,
Shipstead is the place I love."

"What mark did you get?"

"C minus."

"Same here."

"Speaking of Granite," Miguel says. "I hear he's trying to buy Crummie's."

"No way!"

"Wants to own the whole waterfront and build condos and stuff."

"Ach mun, that would be worse than terrible."

"Yummy won't sell," JW says. Yummy Crummie is his mom's best friend. He can't imagine her selling Crummie's.

But the boys aren't convinced. It seems things did sell if there was enough money involved. And Jack Granite, former astronaut and richest guy in town, has more than enough money that was for sure.

The boys go back to pushing their bikes.

"We should build a rope tow on Harper," JW suggests. "Charge kids to pull them up."

"They wouldn't pay," Miguel says.

"They'd be cuttin' the rope," Ty adds.

"Vandalism Costs Everyone," they all say together remembering a billboard in town that didn't last one night before some kid spray-painted:

Creativity Costs Nothing.

Ty turns onto Gardener Ave. "Night guys. Night Janis."

Janis flaps her wing. "Pretty boy! Pretty boy!" she sings out.

"I love you too!" Ty shouts waving.

JW and Miguel both live on Grove St. another four blocks UP.

"What say we stop at Dougie's and see how he's doin' with his no-water toilet?"

"Good idea. Maybe we can help."

JW and Miguel leave their bikes out on the sidewalk and walk softly along the side of Dougie's house. JW says *shhhh* to Janis and she bobs her head. When they get to the wooden picket fence they crouch down and look through the slats. Douglas "Don't Call Me Dougie" Brown is in the backyard. He's standing in front of a white toilet that's up in the air balanced on two plastic sawhorses. There's a barbecue propane tank sitting on the grass with a rubber tube running from it to the toilet. They watch as Dougie empties a plastic bag into the bowl. JW has the distinct impression Dougie's shiatsu, Spencer, is contributing to his Inventors' project.

Dougie backs up about six feet away from the toilet. He has a string in his hand. "This time!" yells Dougie giving the string a jerk.

KABOOM!

JW and Miguel duck. When they look up they catch Dougie wiping dog poop off his glasses. The white toilet is lying on the grass in two pieces. A door bangs open.

"Douglas, come in here immediately!"

"Yes, mother."

"Look at the house. It's covered in..." The rest is lost in the slamming of the screen door.

JW likes living in Shipstead, California. Now that he spends every other weekend at his mom's boyfriend's place in San Francisco he appreciates Shipstead all the more. It isn't that he doesn't like the big city, it's just that here in Shipstead he feels like he belongs.

"This is an okay place to live," JW says despite the fact he's still pushing his bike UP the hill.

"As long as you don't drop the ball," both boys say together. This is an old joke in Shipstead. If you drop your ball on one of the up-and-down streets, you might as well go in the house crying.

"Yeah, I like it here," Miguel says. "But it must be cool hanging out with Mark Nash."

Mark Nash is JW's mom's boyfriend. JW refers to him as Mark Nash, Famous Rock Star and Rotten Person. He's not sure about the Rotten Person part but Mark Nash is definitely a Rock Star and definitely RICH. He lives in *the penthouse* in San Francisco. He's nice to JW's mom. There's just something...

"Yeah, he's okay. I just wish..."

"Yeah, I know," Miguel says. "You just wish you had one bedroom instead of two."

2

Recipe for Disaster

It's now 6:55 p.m. on the same October Saturday. JW has finally made it home to 17 Grove St. where he lives with his dad and his twin sisters, Paula and Georgia. They're named after two more of the Beatles, Paul McCartney and George Harrison. It's the twins' thirteenth birthday and they're out back in the hot tub with their four most favorite girlfriends.

Dr. Martin has provided the girls with large plastic glasses of iced tea and floating in the middle of the hot tub is an Island of Snacks complete with miniature palm tree that lights up. The girls are all wearing sunglasses and waving their arms about like movie stars.

JW and Miguel put Janis in her room above the garage then go through the side door into the kitchen looking for cold drinks after their hard climb. Ringo, the three-legged Bernese Mountain dog, thumps his tail in welcome. Dr. Martin pulls his head out of a cupboard.

"Miguel, how's it goin'?"

"Good, Dr. Martin. How 'bout you?"

"Can't complain. How are the animals, JW?"

"Florida is homesick." Florida is the Haycock's cockatoo. She's boarding at *The Pet Vet* for a month while her folks are visiting their daughter in New Zealand.

"Lonely boy!" squawks Dr. Martin.

"Janis told her she was a girl."

"Janis is smart."

"Don't tell her that." JW pats Ringo and looks out the kitchen window. "Twins seem to be having a good time."

"I was told it's been *outstanding*, so far."

Dr. Martin is in the process of making an Angel Food Cake. Already baking in the oven are pizzaburgers, the twins' favorite. Dr. Martin is actually a pretty good cook when he's got time to be. He pours the cake batter into the pan and licks the spoon.

JW leads Miguel upstairs to his bedroom — the twins have named it *Winnemucca* after the famous California landfill site — where JW's goal at the moment is to TRIUMPH at this year's Inventors, thereby stomping on archrival Douglas "Don't Call Me Dougie" Brown, who won last year by creating the Milky Way in a Coke Bottle.

JW's about to let Miguel in on his secret project but first JW is forced to deal with a distraction in the form of a three-and-a-half foot high blue-butted baboon who is wearing JW's underwear.

All of it.

"Eric, put that stuff back," JW says.

JW decided some time ago there had to be a worse fate than living with a blue-butted baboon, but right now he can't imagine what it could be unless it was living with two blue-butted baboons. And even that couldn't be much worse than living with *this* one.

At the moment, Eric Burdon, this is the baboon's name, is prancing around Winnemucca wearing on his head JW's *favorite* boxer shorts, the bright yellow ones with the Hawaiian hula girls. In his right hand Eric is twirling JW's *second favorite* boxer shorts, the red ones with the pink flying pigs, and on his left arm Eric Burdon proudly displays, like a watch salesman, the rest of JW's underwear drawer.

To sum up, Eric is wearing underwear everywhere but where you're supposed to wear it. And Miguel laughing isn't helping the situation.

"Put that stuff back!" JW says again but it's too late. Eric Burdon swings out of the open window, latches onto the fireman's pole, and slides effortlessly down to the deck below where he is greeted with shrieks of laughter from the SIX HOLLYWOOD STARLETS in the hot tub.

"Do your funny dance, Eric," Paula says grinning up at JW and Miguel standing in the window. She waves. Miguel waves back.

Eric Burdon starts into his crowd pleaser, *The Funny Dance*, which is a mixture of Egyptian Hieroglyphics and Lady Gaga. This time it's made even funnier by the addition of JW's underwear. JW sighs. Living with twin sisters can sometimes be worse than living with a blue-butted baboon, but that's another story.

"Okay, but you can't tell anybody," JW says.

"Promise," Miguel answers trying to look serious.

Miguel doesn't know a Bunsen burner from a barbecue so JW's not worried about him stealing his idea, he's more worried that Miguel will tell someone who'll tell Dougie.

"Okay, so you know how *Dougie* won Inventors last year by creating the Milky Way in a Coke Bottle?" Miguel nods. He knows JW hated losing to *Dougie*.

"So this year I know I have to do something *really* far out to beat him."

Miguel doesn't think it will take much to beat a blown-up toilet but decides this isn't what JW wants to hear. JW continues.

"So here's my idea. What if, millions of years ago, before there was life on earth, what if an asteroid shower hit the earth? And what if, in one of those asteroids, there was a living cell from another planet?"

"Cool," Miguel says.

JW is walking around his room, at least those parts of Winnemucca where he can walk without stepping on stuff. He's getting worked up about this.

"So, last week, when I was at mom's in SF, I found this store called Weird Stuff."

"Cool."

"It's got things like Moon Rocks, Used Pet Rocks, Pieces of the Berlin Wall, Elvis Sightings, Celebrity Farts, *even* UFO Landing Lights."

"Cool."

"So anyway, I'm wandering around looking at all this neat stuff when I find this bin of Asteroid Bits, Guaranteed Genuine."

"Cool."

"So I bought the biggest one." JW goes to his desk and rummages around. He comes back to Miguel and hands him the piece of Guaranteed Asteroid. Miguel studies it. It looks like a piece of old highway to him but he decides JW probably doesn't want to hear this either.

"Way cool."

Miguel's mom texts. He has to go home which is probably just as well. JW was getting to the tricky part and he didn't think Miguel was going to be much help with that. Dougie Brown could probably help but JW certainly wasn't going to ask him.

JW digs around till he finds his hot plate. He plugs that in and then digs around some more till he finds the large glass beaker. He makes sure that's clean and then flings things around till he finds the big bottle of Diet Coke he's been saving for this. He pours the Coke into the beaker and sets the beaker on the hot plate.

So far, so good.

Here comes the tricky part.

IF there is a living cell from another planet trapped in the piece of Guaranteed Asteroid, and if JW can release it into the Diet Coke, it will be, let's be honest now, it will be less than *outstanding*. Probably a dinky little single cell only visible under the strongest of microscopes. This is not going to blow Douglas "Don't Call Me Dougie" Brown's socks off.

So what JW needs is a way to skip a million years of evolution and end up with — not a dinky little single cell — but a large complex organism never before seen on Earth.

In short, an *Alien Being*.

JW was making brownies last Tuesday when an idea grabbed him by the boxer shorts and yanked. He was reading the side of the brownie box trying to figure out what to do next when he read the words *add an egg*. Of course! That's it! ADD AN EGG! That might be the way to pole-vault evolution.

But what egg should he add?

At breakfast the next morning he asked his dad.

"Hey dad, what would be the oldest kind of egg?"

"They have hundred-year-old eggs in China but I don't think you'd want to eat one. They cook them in manure. They're green inside."

"No, I mean what's the oldest animal we have that lays eggs?"

"You mean like dinosaurs?"

"Dad, I hate to break it to you but we don't have dinosaurs."

"My first grade teacher always used to say if someone asked us which came first the chicken or the egg, we should answer the egg because dinosaurs were laying them way before there were chickens."

"Dad, that's the eighty-third time you've told me that."

"Oh... well... I suppose so... let's see, oldest egg... I would say either the Galapagos Tortoise Egg or the Guinea Hen Egg... the tortoise egg is probably protected but I know a farmer with guinea hens. I gather you want several of these eggs if I can get them?"

"Yes please."

It's now 7:15 pm. on the same October Saturday and things are going as planned at the Martin residence until two things happen at once.

The front doorbell rings at the same time as the phone. Dr. Martin looks at the door, then at the phone, then at his Angel Food Cake Batter, the one with all the little polka dots of color. Confetti. The twins' favorite. With butter icing.

Dr. Martin sighs. He should have disconnected the phone and the doorbell, but then he wouldn't be Dr. Martin, *he's so nice.* He picks up the phone which is on its last ring. "Hold on," he says putting it down on the windowsill and heads towards the door where the bell is ringing again.

At the door are Yummy Crummie and her-eight-year old daughter, Amanda. In Amanda's arms is Eddie, Amanda's pug. The dictionary says a pug is *a breed of dog characterized by a short square body, upturned nose, curled tail, and short smooth coat.*

In other words, UGLY.

In Dr. Martin's estimation Eddie is probably THE MOST UGLY DOG in Shipstead but little Amanda doesn't think this and Dr. Martin, *he's so nice,* would never say so. But he thinks it and can now add to MOST UGLY the added blemish of: HAS ROTTEN TIMING.

Eddie is wrapped in a blue towel and it would be hard to miss the dark red patch at his back end. Or the whimpering. Or that Amanda is covered in tears. "He's been hit by a car," she sobs. Dr. Martin looks over at Yummy. Now tears are coming from her eyes too.

For an instant Dr. Martin sees Superman circling Earth reversing time. Not going to happen.

"Go to the clinic, I'll be right there." Amanda turns. Yummy whispers, "Thank you."

JW watches as Eric puts the underwear back in the drawer. JW will say that for blue-butted baboons. There are times when they are *more than nice.* Eric comes over and gives JW a hug.

"Yes, you were very funny Eric, but in future, I want you to know girls' underwear is way funnier than boys'. Now go take Mick

a drink or something. Beat it. Go. Vamoose. I have important work
to do here."

JW now has four of the five ingredients he needs to make an
Alien Being and WIN Inventors. The ingredients he has are Diet
Coke, Heat, Asteroid (Guaranteed) and Guinea Hen Egg. The fifth
ingredient, No More Interruptions, he doesn't have.

"JW!" yells Dr. Martin heading back to the kitchen. JW is about
to break open the guinea hen egg and start *Alpha Amoeba, Quest for
Life.* This is the name he's given to his project. He puts the guinea
hen egg back in its carton and heads downstairs.

"I've got to go to the clinic," his dad says. "Eddie's been mangled
by a car. You're in charge. The pizzaburgers are in the oven and
should come out NOW. Put them on that big round plate and do not
accidentally dump them in the hot tub." Dr. Martin takes the time
to make eye contact with his son.

"This is the twins' birthday. Don't screw it up."

JW nods.

"Then put the cake in the oven and set the timer to whatever
the box says. The icing recipe is in *Joy of Cooking.* Butter Icing. All
the ingredients are here."

More eye contact.

"I'll phone you from the clinic and tell you how long I'll be.
Maybe I can still make the Lighting of Candles."

And with that Dr. Martin is gone.

Does this sound like a Recipe for Disaster?

It should, it is.

3

Where There's Smoke

JW successfully removes the pizzaburgers from the oven and successfully delivers them to the hot tub.

"Where's dad?" Georgia asks. JW watches as six dripping girl hands descend on the pizzaburgers.

"Eddie got hit by a car. Dad's gone to the clinic."

This is *so a part* of the Martin kids' lives that they don't think twice about it. If somebody needs help their dad will help. End of story. Their mom thought it was the end of the story too but she didn't like the ending.

"Just once," she'd say, "I'd like to come first."

Dr. Martin would argue but in the end he knew she was right; he could never say no to an animal in need. Then one day JW's mom — Cynthia — pregnant with a fourth child, another boy, felt something break inside and instantly she knew the baby was in trouble. She called her husband but Dr. Martin was a hundred miles away dealing with an irate Orangutan. By the time Cynthia got to the hospital it was too late. Dr. Martin arrived as quickly as he could but when he saw the sadness in his wife's eyes he knew it was too late for him as well. Something had broken between them and try as he might Dr. Martin could never repair the damage. Cynthia took to spending much of her time alone, much of it driving up and down the Pacific Coast Highway almost as if she might find her baby lying beside the road.

Then one day, about a year later, Mrs. Martin's ancient Mazda broke down on the PCH and who should pull over to help but Mark Nash, Famous Rock Star and Rotten Person, cruisin' the highway in his brand new metallic black Ferrari. It was love at first sight which was surprising on both counts because Cynthia had assumed she was still in love with Dr. Martin and Mark Nash had decided — after two messy divorces — he'd rather make money singing about love than be *in it*.

Cynthia got the car fixed and returned home. She tried to make IT work for the kids but things just weren't the same. She kept feeling the rush of wind in her hair, she kept smelling the leather of the new seats and her lips kept tingling with memories of the one kiss she and Mark Nash had allowed themselves.

Two months later, she and her things were in San Francisco sharing *the penthouse* with Mark Nash, Famous Rock Star and Rotten Person.

How cool was that?

JW comes back into the kitchen, puts the cake in the oven, sets the timer (25 minutes at 350°) and opens *The Joy of Cooking*. ICINGS see Cake Icings. JW scans the B's. No Butter Icing. Brown sugar, quick; Butterscotch. Nothing in between. Great. This is so like his dad.

Words come out of his dad's mouth but his brain is so far ahead of the words he often skips ten sentences and leaves you to figure out how he went from saying "there are less than 650 mountain gorillas left in the world" to "take out the recycle bin."

Now what? thinks JW. There's no point calling the clinic he'd just get the machine. The twins are no help. They think a *spatula* is some kind of deadly spider. Mrs. Bayley, that's what! Gloria Bayley is JW's girlfriend and her mom is a great cook. She'll know the recipe from the ingredients on the counter. JW reaches for the phone but it isn't in its holder it's lying sideways on the windowsill. The red light is on.

Oh boy.

"Hello?" JW can tell by the hollow noise his voice makes that he's on a speakerphone.

"That you, JW? Mark Nash here. I was beginning to think the ol' place had burned down. Hold on, I'll get your mom." JW can hear high heels coming across wooden floor.

"JW?"

"Hi, mom."

"How are you?"

"Good. Hold on, I'll get P&G."

His mom is still talking but he hasn't forgiven her yet for leaving. He doesn't think he ever will. He carries the cordless out to the deck and hands it to Georgia.

"It's mom."

He returns to the kitchen. Now what? There are still twenty minutes on the timer. Time to bike over to Gloria's house, she lives three minutes away, ask her mom and get back. He stares out the window watching his sister Georgia telling her mom *everything*. Out of the corner of his eye he sees movement behind the cedar hedge at the back of the yard.

JW can see three boys, the twins' age. Billy Ridout, Juan Crerar, and the third will be *Spike* Lee, that was a given. And up to no good, that was another given thinks JW. Probably going to sneak under the deck and drain the hot tub. JW considers yelling at them but what fun would that be?

JW looks across the yard to where ZZ Top, the baby komodo dragon, is sleeping in his enclosure. There is no way JW can let ZZ loose without being seen.

This situation calls for drastic measures. JW goes to the backroom where Gerry is stretched out in his wire cage. JW opens the door and calls to him.

"Hey Gerry, show time!"

The three boys are down on their bellies getting ready to crawl from the cedar hedge to the deck when Gerry comes rolling down the hill. On a List of Positions to be in when Meeting an Eight-Foot-Long Ball Python, being *On Your Belly* is probably right at the bottom with *Sitting On Toilet*.

The boys certainly think so. Gerry unravels right before their eyes. Gerry opens his mouth wide because it's SO EXPECTED. The three boys go from happily crawling forward, this is going to be so good, to full-speed reverse Screaming Maniacs in less time than it takes to say "pee your pants."

By the time JW retrieves Gerry, the boys are six backyards away and still making enough noise to pull people from their televisions. It's very satisfying. JW is tempted to drop Gerry in the hot tub but thinks better of it. The twins would tell and besides it's time to show his dad he can do things without screwing them up.

JW puts Gerry back in his cage, rewards him with a "Good job, Gerry" and a snake biscuit. (Let's just say you won't find the recipe for snake biscuits in *Joy of Cooking*.) That done, JW flips the cage door closed and heads back to the kitchen.

And the cage door would have closed if Gerry hadn't flicked his tail at the last second.

On purpose.

JW looks at the ingredients on the counter then out to the hot tub. Now Paula is on the phone telling her Mom *everything*. Who says girls don't have upper body strength? Too bad JW is *between cell phones*, meaning he's lost the one his dad gave him for Christmas (and the two before that.) JW looks at the timer. Twelve minutes. Still time to bike over to Gloria's.

JW goes out the front screen door, down the steps, twirls on the newel post and enters the garage. Mick Jagger, the old lowland gorilla, not to be confused with the 650 endangered mountain gorillas, is sitting in his bamboo-hanging chair staring out at the ocean. Stevie Nicks, the Siamese cat with the air pellet in her brain, is on her pad on the floor stretching.

"Hey Mick, Stevie. How's it goin'?"

Mick waves and Stevie ignores him which is what cats do best. JW grabs his bike and heads UPhill on Harper. Right on Oceanview. Left on Grand. Just three UP blocks to get to Gloria's. That was about right. Any more than that and a boy should probably consider finding another girlfriend. JW chuckles at this. In Shipstead you usually ended up with friends who lived *sideways* from where you lived.

One more block to go. As JW makes the turn onto Gerard he slams on his brakes. There's Gloria standing on her verandah *kissing* another boy. She has her arms around him and they are definitely *kissing*. JW spins around and in two pushes is back on Grand his heart shattered.

It takes JW over half-an-hour to walk his bike home. His eyes are red from not crying and it's only as he drops his bike in the driveway that he remembers the cake. And he only remembers it then because he smells it. And it isn't a good smell, it's a *burnt* smell.

He runs into the kitchen but he knows it's too late because he can't see the stove for the smoke. He grabs an oven mitt, yanks open the oven door, seizes the cake, which is on fire, and pitches it into the sink. He turns the water on and is met by a cloud of steam.

Five minutes later the six Hollywood starlets are still in the hot tub. The cake (Soggy Mess) is still in the sink. The smoke is almost gone. The oven looks like a barbecue but JW has sprayed it with oven cleaner. All he's managed so far. His eyes hurt and his heart is broken but still beating.

The phone rings.

"Hey, JW, how's it goin'?" Dad from the clinic.

"Good."

"Great. I should be home in about 25 minutes. Do you think the twins can hang out that long without cake?"

"Sure."

"You okay? You don't sound so good."

"How's Eddie?"

"His back leg is pretty beat-up but I think I can save it. Yummy's turning out to be quite a nurse. Nothing fazes her and she's nice to look at."

Helen Babiuk is Dr.Martin's regular nurse but she refuses to work weekends and there's as much of Mrs. Babiuk sideways as there is up and down.

"That's great, dad. See ya soon." JW hangs up.

Now what?

JW is heading down Harper like there's No Tomorrow. That's how he feels. *No Tomorrow.* The new Whole Foods store closes at eight and he might just make it. Harper is the steepest street in town and JW hasn't used his brakes once. In fact, this is probably the first time in Shipstead's history that a bicycle has gone down Harper without the use of brakes, the dragging of feet or loud screaming.

JW flies by a souped-up '87 corvette like it's standing still. Now JW is coming up to the corner at Front Street where he *has* to turn because if he doesn't make the turn he's going into the Pacific Ocean with the help of a low seawall that will send him high into the air like something out of Cirque du Soleil.

The traffic light turns yellow with JW still twenty feet away. He never does hit the brakes but leans into the corner so low his elbow almost touches the pavement. He would have made it too if old Mrs. Johnson, the only person in town older than Mrs. Johnson is her mother who turned 105 in May, hadn't chosen that exact moment to open her car door, something she'd been working on for the past ten minutes.

JW jams on his brakes and fishtails into the back of Mrs. Johnson's green '78 Gremlin, flips over his handlebars and lands upside down on her trunk with a thunk! All he can see is twilight 'till Mrs. Johnson's face appears in one corner. She has enough wrinkles for an ironing board.

"How long you been there?" she wants to know.

"I just dropped in," JW says sitting up. Dazed. "What time is it?" He watches Mrs. Johnson frown. She probably doesn't know what year it is let alone the time.

"Two minutes after eight."

JW thanks her, picks up his bike and heads for Whole Foods half a block away. They never close on time.

He rides his bike, which now wobbles horribly, thanks to a bent front wheel, right up to the front door. There on the other side of the door is, who else, but Dougie's younger brother, Ernest "Don't Call Me Ernie" Brown, in the act of turning the key in the door.

He sees JW and grins.

JW knows exactly what's going to happen and his heart would have sunk if there was any place lower for it to go.

"Please Ernest," pleads JW through the glass. "I just need a cake mix. Won't take a second."

Ernie smiles the smile of a mean little kid about to squash a big bug.

"Sorry... We're closed."

"Ernest, please. I'll give you anything you want. You can sit in the cage with Mick. You can hold Gerry. You…"

Ernie walks away.

JW trudges home pushing his bike via Gloria's house and stops long enough to throw a rock through her bedroom window. Broken heart/

broken window. It doesn't help. As he swings onto Grove St. he can see his dad's Jeep Cherokee isn't in the driveway. Mrs. Smith, his next door neighbor, is out front watering her flowers.

"Evening, JW."

"Hi, Mrs. Smith. Would you by any chance have a cake mix I could borrow?"

"I've got one of those already baked Angel Food Cakes. Confetti. That do?"

"That would be fantastic!"

"Hold on, I'll get it. Good thing Mr. Smith hasn't seen it or we'd have a fight on our hands."

Hope Springs Eternal. Famous author, Alexander Pope, wrote that in 1685 in reference to his fifteen-year-old daughter, Hope, who fell into the moat and rescued herself by latching onto the underside of the drawbridge. She went up and down four times before anybody else thought to rescue her.

But the point is she never gave up.

Just like JW. He already has the front of the oven cleaned and the self-cleaning timer is on. Mrs. Smith has not only given him a cake but a container of icing as well which he is busy opening. The phone rings. It's Gloria.

"My dad saw you throw that rock. He's going to call the police. Why…"

JW hangs up. The phone rings again.

"WHO WERE YOU KISSING!?" yells JW into the receiver.

"JW?"

It isn't Gloria it's Heather, his dad's latest Woman Acquaintance not yet elevated to Significant Other but Pending Developments.

"Sorry, Heather, I thought it was somebody else."

"I'm at the Clairmont. Your dad was supposed to meet me here…"

"Omigod Heather, I gotta go!"

JW slams the phone down and runs for the deck.

Too late.

JW watches as all eight feet of Gerry slither into the hot tub. He watches as the six Hollywood starlets erupt like Mt. Etna. He watches as the twins' four most favorite girlfriends take off screaming probably never to be seen at 17 Grove St. again. He watches as the twins storm past in tears, dripping, waving their arms, THEIR LIVES RUINED!

Then he walks back into the kitchen and watches as Eric Burdon, the blue-butted baboon, sticks his hand into the container of icing and smears it on his face like he's going to shave with it. JW watches as Ringo, the three-legged Bernese Mountain dog, finishes off the last of Mrs. Smith's Angel Food Cake (Confetti) and licks his lips. He hears Mrs. Smith scream and knows Gerry is making *a guest appearance*. He hears the phone ring. He hears his dad's Jeep Cherokee pull into the driveway.

JW goes next door to rescue Mrs. Smith.

The kitchen is tidy. The oven will bake again. Eric Burdon has had a shower. Mrs. Smith is fine. "Wait till I tell the Bridge Club." Gerry is sleeping. Big day, y'know. The twins are watching Friday the Thirteenth, Part 37. Their four most favorite girlfriends have returned for the sleepover. JW has told his dad what happened but it sounded pathetic even to JW. He goes to his room.

He hates it when his dad is *disappointed*.

Dr. Martin opens JW's door and looks in.

"That was Gloria's dad. He's not going to phone the police but he expects you to get the window fixed. Tomorrow."

The phone rings again. His dad goes downstairs to get it. Then his dad is running out the door. JW hears the car start and disappear down Grove St.

Heather.

He forgot to tell his dad Heather was waiting at the Clairmont. Great. JW picks up one of the guinea hen eggs and pitches it at his poster/dartboard of Mark Nash, Famous Rock Star and Rotten Person. It hits him right in the face.

"Don't look now Mark, but you've got egg on your face."

But JW knows that really the yoke is on him.

"I'm sorry I broke your window." JW has finally found the courage to call Gloria.

"Why did you do that?"

"I saw you kissing that other guy and I guess I lost it."

"That *other guy* was my cousin Jeffrey, from Toronto. He's on his way home. I was saying goodbye."

"I'm sorry."

"You should've trusted me." Click.

It's after midnight when JW finally gets back to *Project Alpha Amoeba, Quest for Life.* His dad had come home twenty minutes earlier and slammed the screen door, the front door and the bedroom door so you didn't need to be a rocket scientist to know things hadn't gone well with Heather.

JW can hear the twins giggling in the living room downstairs. Everybody knows the last thing that happens at a sleepover is sleep.

The Diet Coke is at 127 degrees Fahrenheit. JW stares at the piece of genuine guaranteed Asteroid which looks more like a piece of old highway than JW cares to admit. He drops it into the warm Coke. He picks up one of the guinea hen eggs and thinks of Douglas "Don't Call Me Dougie" Brown and his slimy brother Ernest "Don't Call Me Ernie" Brown. He'll show them. JW taps the guinea hen egg against the lip of the beaker.

Nothing happens.

He taps harder.

Nothing happens.

He taps *really* hard.

The guinea hen egg finally cracks.

So does the beaker.

JW watches as the warm Coke runs out of the crack, across his desk and drops onto his John Lennon Chuck Taylors, the ones his dad bought him for his birthday.

Very calmly, JW picks up the broken beaker and walks over to the open window. Without stopping he rears back his arm and launches *Project Alpha Amoeba, Quest for Life* back into Outer Space.

JW watches as the beaker, the beaker that held all his hopes and dreams, lands with a splash in the middle of the hot tub.

JW stands at the window for sometime staring into the night sky almost as if the beaker is still winging its way towards the moon. He's like a commuter making the same drive for the thousandth time. He's there but his thoughts are somewhere totally different...

...*Gloria's cousin. Go figure... Remember to buy Mrs. Smith another cake... Fix the bike. Fix the window... Get the beaker out of the hot tub before the girls cut their feet on the glass...*

This last thought is like the final turn into the driveway, it brings JW out of his stupor. He climbs out the window, grabs hold of the fireman's pole his dad has installed for fun and safety, and slides down to the deck. He goes over to the bubbling water and pulls the broken beaker out. He reaches around for the piece of asteroid but can't find it. Forget it!

The beaker goes in the recycle bin and JW goes to bed.

A long Crummie Day is finally laid to rest.

Maybe Not.

4

An Extraordinarily Improbable Object

We're lucky to be here. *The Encyclopedia Britannica* calls Man an Extraordinarily Improbable Object. What that means is here's a cup of chicken noodle soup. See if you can make a person out of it!

No really.

Billions of years ago, a rock, not big but incredibly dense, exploded with a giant KABOOM! Scientists call this *The Big Bang.* Thinking about how the rock got there in the first place and what made it explode can give you a headache. But however IT HAPPENED pieces of the rock flew off in all directions and one of those pieces became our planet Earth.

At first Earth was a ball of flames but eventually it cooled down till the oceans were like Warm Diet Coke. At this point there wasn't anything living which was just as well because there was a ton of Ammonia and Methane hanging around which isn't good if you're trying to breathe. Ammonia makes your eyes sting and Methane is what you smell in Mr. Barber's class when you're sitting beside Fartboy.

But here's the *interesting part.*

Right now at JW's house there's a thunderstorm with big bolts of lightning crashing all around Shipstead and out over the Pacific Ocean. One of these bolts lands within yards of 17 Grove St. JW doesn't wake up but his sisters and their four most favorite girlfriends do. They scream. Then they giggle. Dr. Martin, *he's so nice*, gets out of bed to close windows.

Another bolt hits close enough to the house that all the clocks start flashing and the automatic garage doors go up and down, up and down, and the lights inside the garage flash on and off, on and off, entertaining Mick and Stevie who are easily entertained.

And exactly the same thing happened back when the Earth was covered in Ammonia and Methane. There was a thunderstorm and that burst of electricity was just what was needed to kick start LIFE ITSELF.

If JW was awake not sleeping, looking out his window not dreaming about burnt cake and Gloria, he might see the water in the hot tub change color. Then he might see the water in the hot tub start to leave the hot tub. Then he might see *First Prize* in every Science Fair in the World crawl out of the hot tub and catch its breath.

Or at least take its bearings. As *First Prize* doesn't seem to have a mouth or a nose, the concept of catching one's breath is something it probably isn't concerned with. But it is concerned with *something* because it is obviously agitated. This agitation, this moving around in short bursts, first this way and then that, looks like a young child who has lost his mother. There is genuine concern here, fear and longing.

LO is looking for VE and together they make LOVE.

If JW was still awake and looking out his window he would see, quite simply, a giant JELLYBEAN — it's silver, over five feet tall, luminescent (giving off light), gelatinous (see-through), smooth-coated and agitated. And he would hear a whimpering noise though how whimpering can come from a creature without anything to whimper with is full of wonder. So is a giant Jellybean, but here it is quivering beside the hot tub.

Tears are going to be next except before that happens the newborn Jellybean *smells* something. Its body moves like a bloodhound on a scent. It sniffs around the hot tub though there is no designated sniffer that you can see. It moves as if its whole body is sniffing. The rain is making things difficult.

But it doesn't give up and follows the faint trail across the deck to the wall of the house. It follows the scent up the fireman's pole and through JW's open window. It slides across the floor silently, coming to rest at the side of JW's bed. It raises part of its body enough to look at JW sleeping. It moves closer and sniffs.

Sniff, sniff, sniff.

It likes what it sniffs.

Its body squirms like a dog shaking off water.

It's so excited!

It's found MOMMY!

5

Thirty-Seven Mansions

There are thirty-seven Victorian Mansions in Shipstead, California. All of them have a view of the Pacific Ocean. The largest is at the top of the hill and is called Shipstead House. It has twenty-three rooms and was built in 1887 by the town's founder, Captain Thomas Shipstead, who made a fortune bringing tea to America. Captain Tom's house is now owned by Jack Granite, former astronaut and richest man in town. Except even the richest man in town can be dangerously short of cash as we're about to find out.

"Listen Roman, you think I don't know these things?" Jack Granite says. "You think I sit up here looking down at Shipstead without knowing what's going on? I *am* what's going on."

Jack Granite stops to cool down. He takes a sip of his coffee. He throws the ball for Mantis, his Afghan hound. He looks out at the ocean far below. If this isn't the best view in California it's darn close. He looks back at young Roman. The guy's just a bean counter doing what he's paid to do.

"Sorry, Roman. I'm under a lot of pressure here as you know. Okay, let's recap. We've got everything along the water we want except Crummie's. But without Crummie's everything else doesn't matter because it's in the middle of everything... and so far nothing I've tried with Yummy Crummie has worked."

Jack Granite grins in spite of himself. The last time he tried the famous Granite charm on Yummy Crummie she told him where he could stuff it.

"I offered her *four million* and you know what she said to me?" Jack Granite pours himself another cup of coffee. "She says 'this isn't about money, Jack. It's about having a good place for the kids to hang out. Giving them jobs. It's about protecting this beautiful beach.'" Jack Granite stares at Roman waiting for a reaction. "She says 'sometimes there are more important things than money' and then she points up at the sky and says 'you Jack, of all people, should know that.'"

Roman looks down at the sheets of paper in front of him. Agreeing with Ms. Crummie is probably not the thing to do.

"So Roman, has *he* called?"

Jack Granite can't look at Roman and Roman can't look at Jack Granite. They can both feel the blood leaving their faces.

"Not yet," answers Roman. He keeps staring at his hands. They're trembling.

"How far behind are we?"

"Three days."

"Okay, leave everything to me."

While Jack Granite may have the distinction of owning the largest Victorian mansion in Shipstead, JW's dad has the distinction of owning the *smallest*. But, what Dr. Martin's mansion has that none of the other thirty-six have, is a dead tree sticking out of its garage roof. And if that isn't enough, it has the added bonus of having a three-toed sloth living in the tree. If you're not familiar with a sloth it's basically a monkey that doesn't do anything.

The three-toed sloth's name is Manfred Mann and he shares an upstairs room in the garage with Janis Joplin, the one-winged parrot; Alice Cooper, the blind Scarlet Ibis; and for another couple of weeks five baby raccoons known collectively as The Dave Clark Five.

Dr. Martin, *he's so nice*, has cut a hole in the garage roof and dropped a dead tree down the opening so that Manfred Mann can climb up and look around, if he has the energy.

At the moment Manfred Mann, like Jack Granite, is trying to enjoy the view only there's a problem.

His eyes won't open.

Believe it or not, this is a common problem among sloths. Not just opening eyes but getting anything at all to happen can be a major achievement. Most people think these problems are caused by extreme laziness, *slothfulness*, but that isn't it at all. The real problem is a sloth's brain is split in two and the two halves do not always see eye to eye, so to speak. Here's what happens.

"Yo, Manfred," Mann says. "There's not much point in me opening my eye if you're not going to open the other one."

"My dear Mann," Manfred replies, "perhaps I am not ready to open my eye."

"And pray what are you waiting for?"

"I'm waiting for you to close your eye."

"If I close my eye and you open your eye we'll be right back where we started. One eye open and depth perception worth spit."

"I would like both eyes to open at the *same* time."

"You are something else, Manfred, y'know that?"

Half-an-hour later.

"So, Manfred, is there some signal we're waiting for here? Something that'll tell us when to open our eyes?"

"I thought we might count to three as a way of expediting the situation."

"There wouldn't be no *situation* if you'd just open your eye instead of talkin' about it."

"I was not aware the President was coming for lunch."

"What the heck does that mean?"

"It means you appear to be in a *hurry* for no reason that I am aware of."

"Hurry? If we don't get a move on it will be dark and there won't be anything to see anyway."

"My point exactly."

Half-an-hour later.

"Okay, Manfred. I am counting to three and I expect that eye to open. One, two, three."

"Say please."

"One, two, three, please!"

"There, you see, I am quite willing to co-operate if treated properly."

Half-an-hour later.

"Hey Manfred," Mann says, "what would you think if we *looked around*? Y'know, move our head a little. Side to side. Sweep. Swivel. Up and down. See who's in the backyard messin' with the hose? See what ZZ's up to? Y'know, like, check things out?"

"I am considering your proposal."

"Considering? How 'bout for once we just *do* something without takin' all day to think about it."

"Acting without proper consideration can lead to rash behavior."

"GOOD! LET'S GET A RASH! A RASH COULD BE A GOOD THING. WE COULD ITCH SOMETHING. SCRATCH SOMETHING ELSE. MAYBE WE'D GET A TRIP TO THE CLINIC. RASH COULD DEFINITELY BE A GOOD THING. I VOTE FOR RASH."

"Mann, I want you to know I do not respond well to bullying."

"YOU DO NOT RESPOND WELL TO ANYTHING!"

Half-an-hour later.

"There, are you happy? We are looking *around*."

"Thank you. I'm sorry I yelled at you."

"Apology accepted."

ℭ

It's late Sunday morning, almost noon, and JW isn't doing any better than Manfred Mann but there's a difference. He has one eye open but the other eye is trapped against his pillow and JW is afraid to move *anything* because there is definitely something *not right* in his bed. He can feel it.

Something big is lying along the whole length of his back. So far he's figured out: it's WARM, it's BREATHING, it's STICKY!

JW runs through all the animals in the house and nothing is that big, that warm, that sticky. The only thing close is Gerry covered in raspberry jam and there isn't enough jam in the neighborhood for that.

JW very, very slowly, moves his right hand up till it's resting on his upper leg. Very, very slowly, he moves it backwards till it touches the warm, breathing, sticky thing. This is only helpful in that it tells him what the warm sticky thing isn't. It isn't Gerry covered in jam. It isn't Mick, the gorilla, wearing hair gel. It isn't anything that JW recognizes.

But it's definitely *something*.

If Manfred Mann, the three-toed sloth, woke up to find something sticky on his back he would do what he always does, nothing. The way a sloth looks at things is like this: if I wait long enough the problem will go away. If it doesn't go away I am probably going to be some horrible animal's lunch. Either way the problem is going to go away.

JW has pretty much the same feeling except he decides that if he's going to be something's lunch he wants to at least see what the something is. Without warning JW throws himself off the bed only to find himself a foot above the floor facing the ceiling. Whatever this sticky thing is it's now underneath him, pinning him like a giant glue trap. And it does smell like raspberries.

"Let me go!" JW says.

Knowing what we know, that a huge Jellybean born in the hot tub has JW in his grasp, we would be extremely surprised if the English words "let me go!" had any effect whatsoever.

Well surprise, surprise!

Not only do they have an effect the effect is *immediate*. The Sticky Thing flings JW high into the air. Unfortunately, for JW, gravity returns him to his original position.

STUCK.

JW can hear his dad walking around outside on the deck. There's water running so he's probably filling the hot tub. JW is tempted to call out to him but there's something about his present position that he doesn't want to share with anyone, even his father. It could have something to do with the *Hooters'* boxer shorts he's wearing.

"Let me go!" JW says again.

This time JW is ready and as he's heading for the ceiling he rolls over and looks down. A lot of thoughts can go through a human brain in a short period of time. Here are the four thoughts that JW manages:

It really was a piece of ASTEROID!
I'm going to WIN Inventors!
It looks like a giant BOOGER!
I'm going to land FACE FIRST!

JW puts his hands out to cushion the blow. His hands hit the Booger and keep going. It's an over-used word in such circumstances but it seems the only word for what happens next.

SPLAT!

Words that imitate a sound such as *crack* and *splat* are called onomatopoeia. This is not a word you want to get in a spelling bee.

"llllleeeettttmeeeegggggggooooo!" manages JW drowning in stickiness.

This has no effect but JW trying to kick his legs and wave his arms conveys the message to the giant Jellybean who rolls to the right releasing JW to the floor. He's now trapped between the Booger and his bed. JW wants to run out of the room screaming but lies frozen instead. If the Booger had wanted him for lunch JW would have been a burp hours ago.

JW tilts his head slowly. The Booger seems to be looking at him though what he's using to look with JW has no idea. There isn't anything that looks like an eye, in fact there isn't anything that looks like anything. No eyes, no nose, but he can hear sniffing, no ears but the thing can obviously hear, no mouth but the thing must eat and if it eats it must do those other things, you know, number one and number two. It occurs to JW that maybe Booger has a number three.

He definitely has a skin like a jellybean. He's sort of silver and sort of white and sort of see-through and sort of not. *Sort of not* reminds JW of the word *snot* and as much as he hates to admit it, being the Creator so to speak, Giant Snot is pretty much what we're looking at here. JW isn't complaining. He wanted something different and he got it.

BIG TIME.

There's that smell again but this time it's minty. JW slowly rolls over and props his head on his hand and looks at Booger. With his other hand he points at himself.

"JW." He taps his chest. "JW."

Booger makes no noise but his outer skin seems to give off more light. Then JW has the strangest sensation of a word taking over his brain.

The word is MOMMY.

6

The Care and Feeding
of an Alien Being

JW is dying to tell somebody about Booger. But like Elliott in the movie *E.T.* he's smart enough to know if he does tell that will change everything. His sisters can't keep a secret, that's a given. Neither can Miguel or Ty. Gloria, his ex-girlfriend, probably doesn't want to hear from him about *anything* at the moment, let alone this.

"Hi Gloria, wanta come over and see my giant Booger?"

JW would love to call Dougie but that would be the same as buying a full page advertisement in the *Shipstead Times*.

His dad is the sensible person to tell but that's the trouble. He's sensible. He would want to share this discovery with the world and JW isn't ready for that, yet. But there's Inventors in three weeks. How cool is that?

JW studies Booger and tries to think of a better name. *Jellybean* is too cute, like one of those horrible beanie baby names like *Warm & Fuzzy*. *Hi Ho Silver* seems like something an orthodontist would name his bank account. *Raspberry* has other connotations. *Sticky* and *Snot Burger* are hardly improvements.

Like any new parent JW is going to wrestle with this problem for several days and then give up.

The good news is JW seems to have convinced Booger to stay in his room and play. He's done this by saying "Please stay here 'till I get back." And by closing his eyes and making pictures in his brain of a happy Jellybean happily playing with the happy things in JW's happy room, like the happy racing car set and the happy telescope.

JW shuts the door and heads downstairs. His dad is still out on the deck.

"Morning, JW. Boy, those girls sure kicked the water out of the hot tub. Half empty. I promised the twins I'd take them to *WaterWorld* for their birthday. That interest you?"

JW is about to answer when he sees Booger sliding down the fireman's pole. He fills his brain with *Get back in my room right now!* but Booger keeps coming. Fortunately, Dr. Martin is now preoccupied with watering the flowers.

"I better get Gloria's window fixed."

"That's right. Yes, you better."

JW wraps his arms around Booger — he's light considering how big he is — and pushes him into the hot tub. *Lie on the bottom and don't move* flashes through JW's brain.

"How's your Inventors' project coming along?"

"Not too good. I think I better get another idea."

His dad flips the hose off, turns towards JW. "Never a good idea to put all your *eggs* in one basket," he says chuckling.

The house is quiet. JW and Booger are in the kitchen. Booger is sniffing things.

"Are you hungry?" JW moves his mouth like he's eating. Booger's outer skin glows brighter but that's it. JW opens the fridge, takes out a carton of milk and a bottle of raspberry jam. Booger *has* to love raspberry jam. From the cupboard he gets peanut butter and two plastic glasses. Bread from the breadbox. Booger seems content to watch him.

JW makes two sandwiches and pours two glasses of milk. He puts them on the counter and sits down on a stool. He pats the stool beside him and Booger moves to the stool and sits down.

And down.

Somehow Booger is sitting on the floor and the stool has disappeared inside him. JW can't help but laugh. But Booger isn't defeated he just stretches his body up till he's on a par with JW. Booger watches as JW picks up his sandwich and takes a bite. JW chews, swallows, takes a gulp of milk.

Booger sniffs his sandwich then his glass of milk. JW knows everything is wrong but he doesn't know what to do about it. How can you drink milk from a glass when you have no hand to pick it up with and no mouth to pour it into? Suddenly JW is afraid. What happens if Booger starves to death before Inventors?

JW feels guilty about being so selfish and rethinks his thought to be *Please Booger, eat something.*

With that Booger knocks the glass of milk on the floor. JW watches fascinated as Booger spreads out covering the puddle of milk. JW gets off his stool and walks away a few feet. Booger moves towards him and JW sees that the milk isn't on the floor anymore. Neither is the stool. Oh boy, thinks JW. Better not let Booger sit on the couch.

JW puts the sandwich on the floor and it disappears too. "Is that enough food? Do you want more?" JW has no idea but figures if Booger is hungry he can always eat another stool. Before JW can think what to do next, Ringo, the three-legged Bernese Mountain Dog, comes into the kitchen his peg leg drumming on the floor.

He stops when he sees Booger, then advances sniffing like crazy. Booger is doing the same. Before JW can decide if this coming together is going to be good or bad Ringo walks right into Booger and disappears inside.

"NO BOOGER, NO! DO NOT EAT THE DOG! GIVE HIM BACK. NOW!"

Before JW can set the World Record for Youngest Heart Attack, Ringo limps out the other side of Booger looking none the worse for wear. He comes back around and looks up at JW as if to say where's my peanut butter sandwich? JW makes him one and another for Booger.

RINGO EATEN BY ALIEN. The *National Enquirer* would have loved it.

JW leads the way to the laundry room where Gerry is pretending to be asleep. JW opens Gerry's door and pulls him out, spilling him onto the tile floor. Booger stretches out assuming the same snake shape as Gerry. Gerry raises his head, Booger matches him. Then they both move forward intertwining their bodies, spinning round and round each other like twisting skipping ropes.

Wow, thinks JW, that is so beautiful. If dad was here he'd have the Beatles on, probably *Long Tall Sally*.

Twenty minutes later, JW leads Booger out into the backyard. He's giving Booger a tour. The backyard is full of trees and the neighbors are far enough away that JW isn't worried about Booger being seen. He walks over to the low chain link fence that marks the boundary of ZZ Top's home. ZZ is a *baby* komodo dragon who already weighs over two hundred pounds. JW's dad is trying to find a home for ZZ before he gets much bigger. ZZ lumbers over to the fence.

"ZZ, this is Booger. Booger, ZZ." JW watches as Booger pushes his way through the chain link fence, like cheese through a grater ,and reforms like a big puddle down at ZZ's level. They sniff each other. JW isn't sure what's going on but everybody seems happy enough. JW hears a noise. Eric Burden, the blue-butted baboon, is up the telephone pole talking to Manfred Mann. JW waves and Eric waves back. Manfred Mann doesn't wave but JW thinks he might be smiling.

Last on the tour is the three-car garage or *coach house* as it's called by real estate agents. It's separate from the mansion and bigger than some of the smaller houses in Shipstead. JW brings Booger in the side door away from the street. Mick is swinging in his swing, Stevie is ignoring. JW unlocks the cage door and he and Booger go inside. JW sits in the other swing.

"Hey Mick, this is Booger. He's from another planet, I think. Maybe. I mean he was born here, I guess, but I have no idea what I'm trying to say and you probably aren't getting it anyway. Booger, you sit here for a minute while I try to fix my bike."

JW gets off the swing and motions for Booger to take his place.

"And don't eat the swing."

Booger moves into the swing and this time doesn't fall through. He's catching on. JW wants to open the garage door, Mick loves watching the ocean, the boats going by, the seagulls. At least that's the kind of thing JW sees when he looks at the ocean. Maybe Mick sees something completely different. *Africa, freedom, memories, sunshine.*

Maybe he just likes the warm breeze thinks JW.

Doesn't matter.

What matters is Mick likes the garage door open and JW likes Mick. So JW wants to open the garage door but he doesn't want anyone walking by to see the Gorilla swinging with his new buddy, the Giant Jellybean.

Stevie Nicks picks this time to check out the new guy and jumps up in the swing beside Booger who makes more room for her. JW raises his eyebrows. Stevie isn't known for her friendliness but she seems happy enough beside Booger.

Stevie has an air pellet in her brain — Dr. Martin is afraid to remove it — and once in a while this little piece of metal short-circuits everything and Stevie goes berserk like her tail is on fire. Mick is used to these explosions but JW doesn't think Booger needs one right now.

But JW has other things to worry about like his bike and the big worry, what is he going to do with Booger while he's at Gloria's fixing the window? JW is about to lock the cage when he spies his dad's hot pink overalls hanging on the wall.

Yes, they are his dad's.

Yes, they are *hot pink*.

Yes, they were bought as a joke.

Yes, that's why they're hanging in the garage.

JW goes back in the cage, stands in front of Booger, puts on the overalls. Takes them off and holds them open for Booger. Booger divides in two, fills the legs and stands up. Then he makes two arms and a head that looks remarkably like an oversized guinea hen egg.

Mick gets out of his swing and puts on his *evolution* t-shirt. It too is pink with black drawings showing Man progressing through the ages. The last drawing is of a Woman.

Mick grabs his Giants' baseball hat and puts it on Booger's egg. Booger climbs back in the swing beside Stevie who is laughing. JW is sure of this.

Stevie's probably thinking, *nice hat.*

JW opens the garage door. The sunlight pours in and with it a warm salty breeze. JW's dad has put his old mini-stereo in the garage and has taught Mick how to use it. Mick has a bunch of CDs that people have dropped off for him but his favorite is *The Beatles Live at the BBC* and his favorite track is number nine: *A Shot of Rhythm and Blues.*

Well, if your hands start a-clappin'
And your fingers start a-poppin'
And your feet start a-movin' around...

Mick starts dancing using his black umbrella as a prop. In seconds Booger is beside him learning how to dance. Now Stevie Nicks is thinking, *eat your heart out, John Travolta.*

Or something like that.

7

Things are Different

JW's bike is a mess. The front wheel looks like it was designed by the Snake Department. It's amazing the rubber part is still on. JW looks around. There are other bikes, of course, but the Martins have a rule that no one can borrow anything from the other guy without asking permission and, as JW *is the reason* for this rule, he's hesitant to break it.

He pops the wheel off and stands on it. He puts it on the workbench and hammers it. He puts it in the vice and takes it out again. He puts it back on the bike and tries Vulcan Mind Control. He says bad words, ones he's learned in the schoolyard. He says *really bad words*, these ones from the team bus.

Finally, he looks over at Booger and says, "Nice hat."

Booger slides between the bars of the cage leaving the overalls behind him. He comes to the fallen bike and flows over it. As he comes off the bike he forms his jellybean body into an exact copy of JW's twelve-speed.

Sort of.

To start with the whole bike looks like it's made out of silver see-through plastic that glows. Even the seat and the tires. JW has to admit it's just about the *coolest* thing he's ever seen.

And that's a problem. If he rides Bicycle Booger the way it looks now, assuming Bicycle Booger actually works, every kid in Shipstead is going to be right on his tail asking where he got it.

"I don't suppose," JW says, "there's anyway you could be a

different color, like black? See, black, like this tire."

We really shouldn't be amazed when The Kid from the Hot Tub does it again. JW wants black, black is what he gets. Shiny black like a bowling ball.

"Whoa!" JW cries grabbing a handlebar, pulling Bicycle Booger to his feet, so to speak.

"Whoa!" he cries again.

JW climbs aboard and slowly lowers himself onto the seat. It holds. He pushes forward and the wheels turn. Booger's even smart enough not to have copied the crumples in JW's front wheel. The steering works. JW squeezes the brakes and nothing happens.

Doesn't matter, it's UPhill to Gloria's anyway. JW is so happy he laughs out loud. Not only has he got wheels, he's got Booger *right* where he wants him.

Every kid in Shipstead knows if you have to go UPhill you'd better be going as fast as you can go before you make the turn. That's why when JW leans into the turn onto Harper, he and Bicycle Booger are *flying*.

The other thing that every kid in Shipstead knows is that when your bike is no longer going forward it's a really good idea to jump off. Otherwise you're liable to end up in the Pacific Ocean going backwards faster than a turkey before Thanksgiving. In Shipstead there's no disgrace in walking your bike UP a hill. Rich kids do it, bullies do it, JW does it, even Greg LeMonde, first American to win the Tour de France, does it.

But not today. Today many things are going to be *different* and this is one of them. JW turns the corner onto Harper and never slows down. He feels like Superman rushing to rescue Lois Lane. Like Luke Skywalker on a speeder bike. Like Harry Potter chasing the Golden Snitch. Those are the feelings for the first UPhill block.

The feelings for the second UPhill block are somewhat different.

Remember how Booger was smart enough not to duplicate JW's wonky front tire, well, he's also smart enough to see that there are certain design improvements that could be made to the primitive bicycle.

For instance, what would happen if the back wheel suddenly grew twice as large as the one in front?

We could ask JW this question because he is currently riding just such a bicycle. Can you see it? JW isn't riding uphill anymore; it's as if he's on flat ground. Which would be a very interesting concept as long as nobody else sees him.

"Booger, we're trying to be *inconspicuous* not circus entertainers!"

This has the desired effect, sort of. The back wheel returns to its normal size but now the front tire turns into something resembling a black basketball. JW is flat again, just as conspicuous and even more stupid looking than before.

"Booger!"

Every child has to go through a rebellious period and Booger isn't about to kowtow to arbitrary parental guidance without trying at least one more idea. How about a bike with a back tire *four* times the size of normal? Whoa, up goes JW like he's riding one of those reverse roller coasters.

Now JW is so far off the ground he's leaning downhill even though he's going UPhill!

"BOOGER!"

Bang! The Bicycle Booger crashes back to normal.

BORING MOMMY is the thought that now floods JW's brain. He makes the turn onto Oceanview. JW looks back. No witnesses that he can see. Nobody pointing. No little kid running to get his father.

Yep, thinks JW, there's only one thing to worry about and that would be the police car with the flashing red lights pulling up beside me. JW stops and so does the cruiser. The policeman leans out of his window.

"JW, that's some kinda bike you got there."

"Yes, sir."

The cop is Sheriff Riley who's a regular at *The Pet Vet*. His cat Macavity is prone to toothaches.

"I've never seen a bike could make its wheels go up and down like that. How do you do that?"

Do you know the word *dumbstruck*? It means your brain takes a vacation. You're in Shipstead, California, but your brain is in Hawaii catching a few rays. Lying on the beach. Watching the girl brains go by. Dark clouds, might be a brain storm later...

"JW?"

"Oh, I... you... just turn this handle grip and..." JW rotates his right hand hoping nothing will happen. No such luck. The back wheel grows until JW is facing straight down. He wants to yell BOOGER! as loud as he can but is afraid Sheriff Riley will think he's yelling at him. Calling a policeman *Booger* is probably not a good idea.

JW is in danger of going right over when he thinks to turn the handle grip the other way. The back wheel shrinks to normal. JW rotates his left hand and the front wheel grows. He stops it and grows the back wheel to match. He's so far up he looks like a skinny monster truck.

Shrink the front, grow the back, grow the back, shrink the front. Next thing you know JW is out the chute riding Bucking Bronco Booger, the hottest ride this side of Albuquerque. Ride'em cowboy!

"JW, that's the craziest thing I ever saw."

Fortunately for JW his brain has caught a limo from the airport.

"Actually, Sheriff Riley, this is my Inventors' project. It's supposed to be a secret. I'd really appreciate it if you didn't tell anyone about this."

"JW, they wouldn't believe me anyhow."

As JW turns onto Harper two thoughts occur to him. One: Booger is less than a day old and already he can communicate, turn himself into a working bicycle and turn that into a bucking bronco that can go UP hills. A day old human baby is doing well to fill its diaper.

Two: Booger is less than a day old and already he's nearly as big as JW. Is he born full-size or is he going to end up with his bottom in the basement and his top in the attic? That wouldn't be good.

JW arrives at Gloria's and the first thing he notices is Douglas "Don't Call Me Dougie" Brown's bicycle lying on the grass. He knows it's Dougie's because it's covered in a million miniature bumper stickers that say nerdy things like, *Why be Normal When You Can Be a Geek?*" Or how about, *If you CAN'T Read this HONK your Horn.*

The next thing he notices is Mr. Bayley standing in front of him with the broken window.

"Douglas and Gloria are out back. Do you want me to call them?"

"That's okay. I should get your window fixed."

"I look forward to it."

Heavy heart. That's what JW is lugging around. Here's the recipe: remove all the happiness from your heart and fill the cavity with sadness, twice as much as your heart can hold.

Booger, on the other hand, has a different problem, one that starts with f and rhymes with *heart*.

JW is walking Bicycle Booger down Harper, the broken window resting on the handlebars and seat, when he catches the first whiff of Booger's trouble. Whiff is perhaps not the right word. BLAST would be more like it. And JW catches this blast the same way you might catch a falling piano. It flattens him.

The only good thing is the smell is SO BAD JW forgets his Heavy Heart in his rush not to drop dead on the spot.

"Oh man, Booger, that is so gross. That is like a thousand-year-old gym bag..."

JW is now dancing around, waving one hand while holding his nose closed with the other.

"...full of two thousand-year-old running shoes!"

Fortunately for JW there's usually a sea breeze in Shipstead and this one blows Booger's Blast up the hill towards Gloria's where for one wonderful moment Gloria is convinced Douglas "Don't Call Me Dougie" Brown has filled his shorts.

JW comes back to the scene of the crime and walks Booger into Dead Man's Lookout. Despite the name this is one of the town's most popular parks. There are lots of trees, you can see the ocean and at night it's haunted by sailors' ghosts looking for a tall ship. That's what they say. JW's been here at night and the strangest thing he's seen is policemen not eating donuts.

JW leans Booger and the broken window against one of the lookout benches. He isn't sure how to broach this delicate subject with Booger but another Booger Blast fries anything delicate within fifty yards.

"Listen Booger, I have no idea how to help you with this, but, I think you need to... y'know... get some stuff out of your system... take a load off your mind... maybe do a little *vacuole*." This last word is something JW has learned in Mr. Barber's biology class. It's what amoebas do to get rid of stuff they don't want.

Dead Man's Lookout is also a favorite place to walk dogs and just as JW is wondering what to say next, old Mr. Walensky appears with his large poodle, Cuddles. At *The Pet Vet* they call him Puddles for obvious urinary infectionary reasons.

"JW, you have broken a window?"

"Yes sir. I threw a rock through it."

Mr. Walensky laughs at this.

"You go to the fair, you pay your money to throw balls at targets, you hit nutting. But a rock always finds the window. Let me guess, a girl is involved. Ya?"

"Gloria. I saw her kissing another boy."

"Ah. That happened to me once too."

"What did you do?"

Mr. Walensky sits down on the bench. Cuddles is on a long leash and wanders around the bench so he can sniff JW's bike that smells so interesting.

"I was at the university in Warsaw. The war was just over and everything was rebuilding. I live in a building that was more falling down than standing up. There was a girl I liked, Anna, her name was, she lives above me. There was a hole in the floor and we would talk to each other through this hole."

Mr. Walensky stops as his face screws up and his eyes begin to water.

"Oh that Cuddles. Such farts!"

Mr. Walensky pulls on the leash.

"Cuddles, go and do business."

JW squeezes Booger's handlebar. WATCH THIS thinks JW. Sure enough Cuddles turns in a spiral and then squats to do his business.

"Then one day, I saw Anna kissing a boy at the university. I was very jealous. I went home and covered up the hole."

"What did Anna do?"

"She knocked on my door. She wanted to know why had I covered up the hole? I told her I saw her kissing another boy."

"What did she say then?"

"She didn't say anything. She went back upstairs."

JW couldn't stand it.

"But something must have happened?"

"I learned a lesson, that's what. Anna didn't make me sad, I made myself sad. I was the one who had covered the hole, not Anna. I was the one whose pride was so important I could no longer enjoy talking through the floor with Anna."

"What did you do?"

"I uncovered the hole."

"What did Anna do?"

"She married me."

Mr. Walensky gets up to poop n' scoop. When he turns around his eyes go wide like hubcaps. JW turns and stares too. There on the grass beside the bench, still steaming, is what has to be the WORLD'S LARGEST NUMBER TWO. And right in the middle of it what should be sticking up...

"JW, is that your stool?" asks Mr. Walensky.

We hope you have a Crummie Day,
We hope you have a Crummie Day.
How we love to hear you say,
Oh Man, I've had a Crummie Day!

JW bites into his Crummie burger. The other one he puts on the cement beside his bicycle when no one is looking. Crummie burgers are good. To start with they aren't flat like other burgers. They're fatter in the middle which makes them juicy. And they aren't defrosted. And they aren't cooked ahead of time. And they're made of natural beef, no steroids, no antibiotics. And the twins say the Veggie Burgers are the best ever.

The buns (multigrain, organic) are baked fresh everyday at Crummie's. You can smell them a mile away. You put the condiments on yourself. A Crummie Burger ends up exactly as you want it not like someone else thinks you want it.

The fries are great too, blanched then fried, brown and crispy, cut from organic potatoes, sometimes sweet potatoes. The milkshakes are made with Crummie's own homemade ice cream, none of that soft garden hose stuff you get other places. Crummie's even has its own special orange drink they make with fresh squeezed California oranges. If you want that you ask for Sunshine. Moonshine is made from fresh lemons and if you want to screw your face up you order Shoeshine (grapefruit) because it's sour enough to knock your socks off.

Yummy Crummie, her real name is Claire Crummie but everybody calls her Yummy, comes and sits down beside JW. She's JW's mom, Cynthia's, best friend. She's the same age as JW's mom and just as pretty. And smart. And kind. JW likes her a lot.

"JW, you don't smell so good."

JW grins. "I was worse."

"Hard to believe."

JW thinks of the old guy at the hardware store he'd handed the broken window to. That guy was probably out looking for a new location. Since then JW had been in the ocean cleaning himself and the kitchen stool as best he could. JW would like to tell Yummy about Booger but for sure she'd tell JW's mom and that would lead to Mark Nash, Famous Rock Star and Rotten Person.

"I talked to your mom today," Yummy says. "She didn't sound very happy. She misses you guys a lot."

JW thinks about this. If there's a solution he doesn't see it. When in doubt change the subject.

"See that stool?"

"Yep."

"Want to see it disappear?"

"It doesn't smell as bad as you."

JW laughs. He's enjoying this. "Look over there." Yummy does as she's told. JW moves the stool beside Bicycle Booger. Now you see it, now you don't.

And don't ask how Booger does it.

It's his *little secret*.

8

How Janis Joplin
Comes to Live at Grove St.

One day, five years ago, Fred Langton, the manager of the local Society for the Prevention of Cruelty to Animals, appeared at *The Pet Vet* carrying a cardboard box and in the box was a mess of bright green and yellow feathers covered in blood. Dr. Martin gently picked up what was left of a parrot. It was breathing, but barely. He made a face and looked at Fred for an explanation.

"Apparently she said 'You old hag,' one too many times."

Dr. Martin couldn't save the one wing but he patched up everything else. If the parrot survived the night she'd mend. Dr. Martin brought the patient home to show the kids and so he could keep an eye on her.

Georgia was the most interested. She went online and proceeded to inform the others that there were over 300 different kinds of parrots. The one in the box was a Yellow-Headed Amazon. Notice the two toes going frontward and the two toes going backwards. The parrot could use these to hold its food. It would like to eat buds, fruits, nuts and seeds. And some parrots lived to be 50-years-old.

"Fifty! How old is this one, dad?"

Dr. Martin thought about this.

"It's really hard to tell how old a bird is. There are no outward signs but you can get an idea by watching how a bird moves. Like the difference between a young dog and an older dog. I have a feeling this one isn't young and isn't old, something in between."

"And it says the Yellow-Headed Amazon is one of the best at talking."

"This one was too good. She called the drunk who owned her 'an old hag' and she threw her across the room."

Georgia reached into the box and stroked the parrot's feathers.

"What are you going to name her?"

Dr. Martin had the job of choosing names because he'd named the first animals after rock n' roll stars he knew when he was a kid. Now it was a tradition.

"Janis Joplin."

"Who?"

Saying "Who?" was also a tradition, one that made Dr. Martin realize he wasn't eighteen anymore.

"Janis Joplin was a great singer with a wonderful raspy voice." Dr. Martin sang a few lines of *Me and Bobby McGee*. The kids made faces which was also a tradition.

"Okay, bedtime."

Everybody huddled round the box for one more look at the newcomer.

"Hang in there, Janis Joplin."

The parrot turned her head just slightly and said her first words at 17 Grove St.

"Got a cigarette?"

Janis Joplin survived and so does JW.

He returns the window to Gloria's dad. Dougie is gone which is good or JW might have broken the window over his head and had to start over. Gloria doesn't come out to see him but that doesn't bother him as much as it should have. JW has uncovered the hole in the ceiling. Gloria can yell down if she wants to.

He stops in Whole Foods and waves to Ernest "Don't Call Me Ernie" Brown as he's leaving. This seems to perplex Ernie which suits JW just fine. He delivers the cake and icing mix to Mrs. Smith.

JW feeds all the animals at 17 Grove St. At five he and Janis ride down to the *The Pet Vet* and feed the animals there. Eddie still has four legs so little Amanda will be pleased. His dad and the twins get home from *WaterWorld* about nine looking tired but happy. His dad has stopped in to check on Eddie too. He phones Yummy to tell her things are okay. By ten everybody is in bed including Booger.

JW isn't comfortable sharing his bed. It feels weird.

"Tell you what Booger. You take the bed and I'll sleep in this sleeping bag."

Ten minutes later JW feels like a hotdog sharing a bun with another hotdog.

"Booger, there isn't room in here for both of us. You stay here and I'll use the bed."

Ten minutes later.

"Booger, this isn't working for me. How 'bout we each have our own sleeping bag? That'll be fun, right? Like camping out."

Goodnight Booger, I think you're great.
Goodnight MOMMY. I love you.

What girls do in the bathroom for forty-five minutes is one of Life's Little Mysteries. Georgia and Paula finally vacate the kids' upstairs bathroom and JW stumbles in followed by Booger. Booger isn't supposed to be following but there are some things Booger chooses not to understand. Anything that takes him away from MOMMY might as well be in Japanese.

This bathroom, like every other room in the house, is decorated in Beatlemania. There must be fifty framed black and white photos of the Beatles around the walls. Some of them signed. JW's favorite is the one of John and Paul singing together in Liverpool. Pete Best, not Ringo, is the drummer and on his drum it says *Silver Beatles*.

JW turns on the shower. The only good thing about being second in the bathroom is you don't have to wait two minutes for the hot water to arrive. On the other hand having hot water doesn't amount to much if there's a giant jellybean between you and the showerhead.

"Okay, you first," says JW.

There's another photo JW likes. It shows the four Beatles standing together in a fog at night by a lamppost. In the white fog is written in black ink, "To the *other* George Martin, love John, Paul, George and Ringo."

That's why the mansion is covered in Beatle artifacts and why the kids are named after the Beatles and why their dad is one of the biggest Beatles' fans on the planet. Because their dad's name is George Martin, and George Martin is the name of the guy who was in charge of arranging and recording all the Beatles' songs. He's now *Sir* George Martin.

And because JW's dad met the Beatles in Liverpool when he was a teenager.

JW looks in the shower. Booger is lying down. Georgia's little yellow Rubber Ducky is floating in a lake Booger has made where his bellybutton would be if he had one.

"My turn."

JW puts his backpack down on the floor under the kitchen counter. This would be a *Booger* Backpack.

"Hey dad, can I borrow your bike?"

"Sure."

JW watches as his dad kisses his sisters on the hair. Dr. Martin squeezes JW's shoulder and heads out the door. We haven't spent much time with the twins so far, because they aren't a big part of this story even though they're a big part of JW's life. He loves his sisters but they drive him crazy. He can even tell them apart which is more than most. Even their four most favorite girlfriends, Uriah, Penny, Izzy and Erica don't always get it right.

"So," JW says "is GUPPIE going to be at the game?" GUPPIE is what JW calls Georgia and Paula and their four most favorite girlfriends. It's the first letter of their first names put together in the worst possible way.

"Yes, TOILETBOY, we'll be there."

It's this kind of warm repartee that brings siblings together later in life.

"JW, do you know where the raspberry jam is?"

Georgia is saying this on her tiptoes looking in a cupboard knowing her big brother will come to her rescue. He does. Meanwhile, Paula is underneath the counter putting an unidentified object in JW's backpack.

The backpack seems different somehow but Paula isn't the kind to worry about details when she could be thinking about herself. In goes the *something*. Stand up. Big Brother is still searching for the raspberry jam that he isn't ever going to find.

Mission accomplished the twins head for the door.

"Forget the jam. See ya, JW. Good luck at the game."

"Thanks."

JW puts a big bowl of Honey Nut Cheerios on the floor beside Booger. Ringo starts for it but Booger is on top of it before Ringo can even lick his lips. JW still has no idea how much food Booger needs. After yesterday's episode in the park he's afraid to take Booger to school. But he's more afraid to leave Booger at home, besides which Booger wouldn't stay anyway.

So Booger is a backpack and Shipstead High here we come! Shipstead High, the boys call it Shipstead Thigh, because the girls are all wearing mini-skirts this year, isn't new. Granite High, the other high school in town, is new. It's in the modern part of Shipstead, a big part of which was developed by Jack Granite, former astronaut turned real estate tycoon.

Jack Granite donated the land for the new school as well as his name. On the other hand, old Shipstead High, all three stories of it, is halfway up the hill settled amid Victorian houses like a mother hen looking after her chicks. Anybody who grew up in Shipstead went to Shipstead High so it has a huge alumni that likes to cheer.

The trouble is ever since Granite High was built there hasn't been much to cheer about. Take the boys' varsity basketball team for example. They haven't beaten their cross-town rivals in over three years.

JW is on the team though he's rarely a starter. Like everybody at Shipstead High he hates losing to Granite but so far hasn't managed to do anything about it. But, as we've learned, Hope Springs Eternal (dunk, dunk) and there's a game this afternoon.

JW sits down beside Gloria. It's math class. Dougie isn't in this class. As you go through life you learn to label things with names like Minor Miracle, Just Desserts, Sour Grapes, Big Deal, No Big Deal, Can of Worms, etc. Another of these labels is Small Mercy. *Dougie* not being in math class is a Small Mercy.

JW swings his Booger Backpack down beside his seat. He looks over at Gloria. She looks at him but doesn't smile. This is called giving him *the cold shoulder* as opposed to *a warm shoulder to cry on*. Then her overly-plucked eyebrows crash together as she shifts her gaze to JW's feet.

JW's backpack is definitely changing colors. It was navy blue when he sat down and now it looks like a piece of sky with a cloud sailing by. If Gloria looked out the window behind her she'd see exactly the same thing.

JW kicks Booger, bends down.

"Stop it," he whispers.

Booger stops changing colors. He's now lime green, the same color as Niki Sanjay's mini-skirt. JW pulls on the backpack zipper which makes a ripping noise loud enough to compete with the school intercom. Gloria frowns again.

"...and don't forget there's a big basketball game today at four against Granite. Let's go you *Tea Merchants*!"

Tea Merchants?

The teams in JW's league are named: the Jaguars, the Raiders, the Marauders, the Hornets, the Eagles and the *Tea Merchants*.

Maybe it sounded okay in 1897 when the school was built.

Go you *Tea Merchants*! Go you *Coffee Purveyors*! Go you *Donut Dunkers*!

Maybe it stunk even then.

JW reaches into his pack and would like to pull out his math notebook except it appears to be stuck to the bottom.

Don't do this Booger.

JW looks inside and sees, besides books and notebooks, a bottle of raspberry jam on its side with no lid.

The Twins Strike Again!

Actually, it's hard for JW not to find this funny. On Friday he put mousetraps in his t-shirt drawer and caught both sisters and Eric Burdon. Because JW helps out at *The Pet Vet* he has money to fix windows and buy cookies. The cookies he hides in his room on the off chance he might actually get to eat a few of them. He caught the girls but they still ate all his Double Stuf Oreos.

JW studies his raspberry jam covered notebook. If he can cut off the bottom half inch he'll be okay.

"Can I borrow your scissors?" JW says this to Gloria but it's Niki who hands him hers.

JW hasn't seen Niki since Janis Joplin squawked "your mother wears army boots." He looks into her eyes and she looks back. Some words are never spoken but understood just the same:

I'm sorry the parrot said that, telepaths JW.

I shouldn't have reacted that way, sends back Niki.

It must have hit a sore spot.

Maybe if we get to be friends I'll tell you about it.

Sorry.

Me too.

Let's start over.

Okay.

JW reaches in to cut the jam from his notebook but the jam is gone. He pulls his book out and hands the scissors back to Niki.

"Thanks."

Niki smiles. She probably lives five blocks UP, but with the Bicycle Booger all things are possible.

While JW is dealing with jam in Shipstead, in San Francisco JW's mother, Cynthia, is lying on her bed bawling her eyes out. Mark Nash, Famous Rock Star and Rotten Person appears in the doorway carrying two mugs of herbal tea.

"Honey, what's the matter?"

"I *gulp sob gulp* miss *sob gulp* the *sob* kids *gulp*."

This admission has been coming for sometime. Like a ship on the horizon, Mark Nash knew one day it would pull into the harbor. But he loves Cynthia and isn't about to lose her now.

"Okay, leave everything to me."

Where have we heard that before?

Jack Granite has a pain in his gut and it won't go away. It feels like someone is twisting his stomach, like you'd twist a dishrag to get the water out. Jack Granite has had stress before but never like this.

He looks down at Shipstead spread out below him. He could be on the Almalfi coast in Italy the way all the pretty white buildings hug the steep hillside and the dazzling dark blue ocean, dotted with sailboats, disappears into the empty blue sky. Two years ago Jack Granite had enough money to retire, enough money never to worry about money again, but it hadn't been enough. He'd wanted more and now he was paying the price for that greed.

Jack Granite's phone rings. He looks at the number calling him. He wishes he hadn't.

"Morning Max... Yes, it's a beautiful day... Yes I know I should have called. I was waiting till I had good news... I offered her four million... She said she'd think about it."

This isn't true. Yummy isn't the least bit interested in selling Crummie's.

"The private detective didn't find anything. She's clean. Lives with her daughter in a little house near the old high school. Husband's dead."

Jack Granite listens to the voice at the other end. It sounds like a gravel truck unloading. Jack Granite's stomach takes another twist.

"We don't need any of that," says Jack. "Give me a few more days. I'm sure I can talk her into selling."

Jack Granite wants to hang up but can't. The voice continues with suggestions of what can be done to force Yummy to sell. Jack feels his California tan leaving his face like coffee poured down a kitchen sink.

"None of that will be necessary. Give me a few more days."

Jack Granite spends the next half-hour staring at Crummie's in the distance below. There must be something he can do to make Yummy sell. Finally Mantis, his Afghan hound, drops his ball onto Jack Granite's shoe and barks. *There must be something.*

⁂

JW's day flies by. Booger behaves himself except for a few seconds in the cafeteria when he takes a shine to a stainless steel garbage can. It has a big domed lid and Booger thinks it might be a relative. Booger stands beside it but he must not have much luck communicating because he's soon back beside JW.

Feeding Booger is easy. JW just drops stuff in the backpack and it disappears. His biology text disappears too but JW isn't sure if someone took it or Booger ate it.

Then it's 3:30 and time to get ready for basketball. The Granite *Marauders* are already warming-up. JW changes and heads out on the court. He looks around for someone to look after his backpack. Gloria is there sitting beside Douglas "Don't Call Me Dougie" Brown. JW doesn't want *Dougie* anywhere near Booger. The GUPPIE are in the back row but Niki Sanjay is upfront.

"Hey Niki, can you watch my bag? Thanks."

JW isn't ever going to make the NBA but he can play. In fact he's having a good enough game Coach doesn't take him out till near the end of the first half. At halftime, Granite is ahead by eight points which is about ten points less than usual.

This is mostly the result of the Granite coach not playing his All-Star guard, Tommy Jones, who is in the doghouse for missing a practice. JW looks over at Niki and smiles. Booger the Backpack is still at her feet behaving himself. Maybe this is all going to work out.

The *Tea Merchants*, feeling good about themselves, come out driving in the second half. JW hits three in a row and Ty, Shipstead's center, scores ten points in three minutes. When the buzzer sounds to end the third quarter Shipstead High holds a slim two-point lead. Their fans, more used to groaning than cheering, finally have something to be noisy about and the Shipstead cheerleaders make the most of it:

"We're the girls from Shipstead High,
We're here to read your fortunes,
You might as well just head on home,
As try to beat *Tea Merchants*!"

That's it for the Granite Coach. He's convinced himself he's made his point with Tommy Jones and puts him in. In seconds the lead is reversed but the *Tea Merchants* aren't going down without a fight.

With five minutes to go they are only behind by four points but Tommy Jones is starting to get his act together. The Shipstead faithful are still cheering their hearts out, but inside the Groans are warming-up getting ready to come in off the bench.

Then suddenly everything changes again. Tommy Jones can't buy a basket. Everything is close but nothing will go in. Even Devon Summers, Granite's six-foot-five center, misses an easy lay-up. The ball circles the hoop three times but falls aside.

With five seconds to go the *Tea Merchants* are trailing 62 to 64 but they have the ball. Miguel passes it to Ty under the basket. The Granite *Marauders* surround him, their arms up like tree branches. But Ty doesn't go for the foul or the tie. He surprises everyone by passing the ball back to JW who is unguarded behind the three-point line.

JW shoots. The buzzer sounds. The crowd is standing, holding its breath. All eyes watch JW's ball arc towards the basket.

Whoosh!

Shipstead High goes WILD!

9

The Lost and Found

Shipstead High is still buzzing. JW finally takes the time to look over to where Niki is. She's standing up, looking around. She doesn't look happy. JW can see why. His backpack is gone.

"I'm so sorry, JW. I don't know what happened. I'm sure no one took it."

"It's alright, Niki. It'll turn up. Don't worry about it."

Big tears appear in Niki's eyes. JW steps forward and wraps his arms around her. Gloria is staring at him wide-eyed.

"It's okay, honest. It's just a bag."

But it isn't okay and Niki knows it.

"Go get changed," she says. "I'll wait for you."

But there is something JW has to do first. He trots over to where Joe Polly, the old equipment manager, is stuffing basketballs into a big net bag. JW knows what's happened to Booger. He can still feel the stickiness on his hand from the winning basket.

"Hey Joe, hang on a sec."

JW runs his hand over each ball in the bag.

"Is the game ball in here?"

"Oh, you want the game ball. Bronze it or something, right? Naw, it's not here. Granite took it. It was their ball. They always insist on playing with their ball and I've given up arguing."

JW looks over at the Granite bench but it's deserted. Now what? He runs to the visitors' dressing room but it's empty. He runs out to the parking lot just in time to see the *Marauder* team bus make the turn onto Harper.

Oh Booger.

Niki is waiting for him.

"Have you got your bike here?" JW asks trying to be calm. Niki nods yes. JW has decided not to race over to Granite High. He's decided Booger, being so smart, will figure out how to get home and if not waiting a bit till the Granite players have disappeared will make it easier to find Booger.

"I have to go to my dad's clinic and feed the animals. You could help."

"We could get a burger after. I have money."

JW's mind is racing, his heart is pounding, his skin is on fire. The only thing keeping him from going berserk is the thought that Booger is smart, so so smart.

"JW?"

But JW can't speak. He grabs Niki's hand and pulls her toward the bikes.

Most days JW likes helping out at *The Pet Vet*. When he's there he understands why his dad loves working with animals so much. It's like caring for a child. The animals rely totally on you to make them better. And they appreciate you, are always glad to see you.

JW flips on the lights and is met by a chorus of barks, yelps and meows.

"Lonely Boy!" yells Florida.

Niki looks happier now too. She is such a pretty girl when she smiles, thinks JW. Tall and slim, long black hair held back in a crystal barrette. Her Fijian ancestry gives her smooth light-brown skin and big dark brown eyes.

"See that hose over there?" JW says pointing. "Use that to fill everybody's water bowl. They like it if you talk to them."

"Hi Honey!" Florida says putting on her widest smile. Niki laughs.

JW starts opening cans of assorted foods. As he works he explains to Niki his dad's system of using colored dots.

"A green dot is dry food. A blue dot is wet. Red is a pill. Yellow is ointment. That's Eddie, Yummy's dog. Amanda's really. He got hit by a car. Dad thinks he's The Most Ugly Dog in Shipstead."

"Hey Eddie, don't you listen to him baby," Niki coos. "He's just jealous 'cause he's not little and cuddly like you are."

JW can see by the look on Eddie's face that Niki has made a friend for life. Then JW remembers the look on Gloria's face at the gym as he hugged Niki. He'd made just the opposite.

"Where's Amanda's father?" asks Niki.

"He died before Amanda was born. A construction accident. A wall fell on him."

"Oh, that's so sad."

We hope you have a Crummie Day,
We hope you have a Crummie Day,
How we love to hear you say,
Oh Man, I had a Crummie Day.

"Crummie's is such a cool place," JW says between bites. His mind is a teeter-totter. One minute he's scared for Booger and the next he figures Booger's so smart he's probably at home playing with Eric.

"There wasn't anything like this in Portland," Niki says.

"Is that where you're from?"

"That and a lot of other places."

Niki has put on track pants and a sweatshirt she's borrowed from Yummy. She's called her mom and everything is cool. JW wants to ask about the other places Niki's lived but decides not to. Niki will tell him when she's ready.

"I sure hope Yummy doesn't sell this place."

"Sell it?" JW pretends not to have heard the rumor.

"Yummy was just telling me. Jack Granite is trying to buy it. He wants to build condos all along the beach."

"Ah man, why can't people just leave things alone? He's got all the money in the world already."

"You got Park Place, you want Boardwalk too."

"Not me," JW says.

"You don't have Park Place."

"I don't want Park Place."

After that JW can't put Booger out of his mind. He has to get going. He can see Niki getting sad because she thinks JW is angry at her for losing his bag. JW can see all this but there isn't anything he can do about it. He has to find Booger.

"We should get going," JW says standing up.

"I'm okay. Yummy will give me a ride home. I can get my bike tomorrow." They look at each other. Niki's eyes are wet with tears. "You go ahead."

JW makes a decision. It's the same decision his dad has to make every time a hurt animal interferes with something important.

"Niki, I'm going to tell you something. You can't tell anybody else."

Niki nods, wipes her eyes.

"You know my backpack? It's not a backpack. It's... an Alien Being."

JW can't decide which is worse, having Niki in tears or having Niki in stitches. The tears made him feel bad, the stitches make him feel stupid. They're hurrying up Harper, pushing their bikes, and JW has been telling Niki about Booger since they left Crummie's. She doesn't believe a word he's saying. Thinks he's making it all up. Niki runs up her front steps then turns back.

"I love your story, JW. I'm sorry about your backpack. You played great. Good night."

It isn't a good night. JW races home and races through the house praying Booger has found his way back to 17 Grove St. but there's no Booger. He checks the hot tub and garage, gets back on his dad's bike and heads towards Granite. The school should be open. Shipstead High is open most nights with different community groups and teams.

The lights at Granite are on. JW ditches his bike and runs inside. There are men playing basketball in the gym. Thirty-year olds with squeaky shoes and too much sweat. One team's jerseys say *Cardiac Arrest*. JW recognizes some town cops on the floor.

The other team is called *Corporal Punishment*. Probably guys from Two Rock Coast Guard Station near Petaluma thinks JW. Judging by the bantering back and forth it's a good game. JW walks beside any basketball he can see. He knows Booger will sniff him if he isn't too far away.

Booger where are you?

The equipment room door is open. JW pokes his head in. "Booger? Booger?"

Dougie empties the bag of Spencer poop into the toilet. The toilet is back up on the sawhorses. Duct tape is holding it together. Dougie wrinkles his nose. He hates this part but being a scientist, winner of last year's Inventors, he knows the value of a precise experiment.

"Here Spencer, here boy." Dougie picks up the little dog and sets him on top of the toilet seat. "Good boy. Isn't this fun? You're going to be part of a science experiment. Get ready."

Dougie steps back, pulls the brown paper bag over his head,

the one with the two eyeholes. His eyes stare out through his thick glasses like two little green fish in a bowl. He picks up the string. "This time" Dougie says. "This time!"

He yanks.

The Latchfords have lived beside Mrs. Brown for over ten years. They've gotten used to the Brown boys, Douglas and Ernest, in the same way you'd get used to the smell of a pig farm if you lived beside one and the wind was blowing the wrong way.

At the same time as Dougie pulls the string, Mr. Latchford, Lloyd, a retired plumber, is sitting in his La-Z-Boy watching a replay of Neil Armstrong landing on the moon. Mrs. Latchford, Betty, a retired hairdresser, is standing at the back window looking at her reflection, trying to decide if she likes her new purple highlights. Outside, pieces of brown stuff start plopping into the Latchford's swimming pool. There's a lot of plopping.

Betty Latchford watches Spencer, the little dog from next door, land in the pool with a splash.

"Lloyd?"

"Yes, dear?"

"When they say it's raining cats and dogs, what do they mean exactly?"

There are some kids hanging around out front at Granite High. JW walks over to them.

"Hi guys. Does anybody know where Tommy Jones lives?"

The kids look him over.

"He left his watch at Shipstead. I want to return it."

They look some more. Finally, JW passes some test that only boys understand.

"He's over on Granite Ridge. Yellow house with dark-green trim. You can't miss it."

"There's a net on the garage." This last remark strikes the kids as being very funny. What isn't funny is JW's dad's bike isn't on the grass where JW ditched it. JW can't believe it.

"Ah man, a gym full of cops and somebody steals my bike."

His *dad's* bike.

Remember the rule that no one is allowed to borrow anything in the Martin family without asking? That's because twice before when JW has borrowed his dad's bike it's been stolen.

When something happens for the second time it's called deja vu, which is French for *already seen.*

When something like this happens for the third time it's called Lake Stupid, which is English for REALLY DUMB.

JW is standing on the bottom of Lake Stupid and he knows it.

JW jogs all the way to Granite Ridge. Something is horribly wrong with Booger, he can feel it.

It's dark now. He finds the yellow house with the dark-green trim. It's a nice house and what's even nicer is Tommy Jones is out in the driveway shooting hoops with his mom. There's a street light at the corner of their lot so seeing the basket isn't a problem. JW introduces himself.

"I know who you are," says Tommy Jones. "You guys played okay today."

"That's 'cause you weren't out there much."

"Coach was teaching me a lesson."

Tommy Jones passes the ball to his mom.

"I know this is going to sound crazy," JW says, "but I *really need* to find today's game ball."

"Devon Summers took it. You know him? Plays center. Mean lookin' dude but he's okay if you don't cross him. Lives over on Powell. Number 28. Said he never wanted to see that ball again. Said he was having a fire tonight and that ball was going in it."

JW runs all the way. As soon as he hits Powell he smells smoke. Bad smoke like coming home to the burning cake. *Deja vu.* He can see people moving around in number 28 but the backyard looks empty. The fire is still burning, the coals red hot. He opens the gate.

JW finds Booger huddled in the dark, in the corner of the yard. He's small about a third his normal size.

He's shaking.

His skin is blistered and wet, oozing something that smells like burnt coffee. JW takes off his sweatshirt and gently wraps it around Booger. Then he picks him up, both of them shaking now, JW cradling Booger like a baby.

I'm so sorry Booger.

I love you Mommy.

JW walks out of the backyard and heads home and from his eyes come those tears that only a mother and father can cry.

10

Booger Bounces Back

JW doesn't go to school. He tells his dad he has a lousy headache. Says he'll go later if he feels better. He doesn't tell him about the stolen bike. Maybe he can find it before he has to star in *Lake Stupid.*

Booger is a bit better. It took JW over an hour to walk home last night. He took the least traveled streets hoping to avoid anyone he knew. About halfway home Booger stopped shivering. JW thought Booger fell asleep then but it was just a feeling.

He managed to get Booger upstairs unseen. He put a clean sheet on his bed and gently unwrapped Booger from his cocoon. The sweatshirt was stuck to Booger's skin so he ran some warm water in the tub and lowered Booger in. The sweatshirt came off easily after that.

His dad keeps supplies in the back of his Jeep Cherokee so JW helped himself to two tubes of burn ointment. These he rubbed all over Booger. Then JW put Booger to bed. Covered him with the clean sheet and sat down on the floor his back against the bed, his arm touching his friend.

JW wasn't much of a singer, not like Mark Nash, but he was so filled with happiness at having found Booger alive he had the urge to sing *something.*

Blackbird singing in the dead of night,
Take these broken wings and learn to fly.
All your life
You were only waiting for this moment to arise.

When JW woke in the morning he was still on the floor but there was a blanket on top of him, a pillow under his head and Booger stuck to his back.

Douglas "Don't Call Me Dougie" Brown waddles out his back door. He's missing school too. Winning Inventors is more important.

He's wearing his almost real astronaut's suit, the one he's worn the last four Halloweens. In front of him he's carrying one of those kitchen stools with the metal steps that flip down to make a short ladder. The toilet is back up on the sawhorses. Another roll of duct tape holds it together.

Dougie clunks up the steps and lowers himself onto the toilet seat. Spencer is sitting on the grass looking up at him. Dougie has tied the pull string to Spencer's collar. In his hand he holds a red rubber ball. When he throws the ball Spencer will run after it and that will set off the explosion.

Through the clear plastic visor you can see Dougie's eyes close behind his glasses and then you can see his lips move. "This time," he whispers throwing the ball.

At the moment Dougie throws the ball, Mr. Latchford, Lloyd, is sitting in his La-Z-Boy watching Neil Armstrong land on the moon again. Mrs. Latchford, Betty, is standing at the back window, looking at her reflection, trying to figure out why a permanent wave is called that when it isn't. Outside, in the swimming pool, there is a huge SPLASH! followed by more plopping.

"Lloyd?"

"Yes, dear?"

"An astronaut just splashed down in our pool."

Mark Nash stands at the railing of his balcony and looks out at San Francisco Bay. He's come a long way from his days as a back-up singer for Freddy Fender. Unlike most of the rock stars he knows Mark Nash understands money. Knows how to make it work. And once you learn that there isn't anything you can't do.

Well, that isn't quite true. There are still things money can't buy but it seems like they're getting fewer and farther between all the time. Still, this latest problem is tricky, but Mark Nash being *Mark Nash*, figures money will win in the end.

He looks around to make sure Cynthia is still working out in the weight room, then punches numbers into his BlackBerry.

"Sal, I'm glad I caught you. I've got a problem here. It's Cynthia. She wants to get her kids back.... They're up the coast in Shipstead. The son's fifteen so there's probably nothing we can do there, but the two girls just turned thirteen .... yeah, they're twins... naw, they're in school there, friends are there...yeah, I could get a place there maybe have the girls half the time but I'd rather stay here...yeah... but nothing too bad or it'll slop over onto the kids... Why don't you go up there and check it out? Okay, ciao."

Niki calls JW at lunchtime. "Are you okay? Georgia says you have a headache."

"I'm okay."

"Did you find Booger?" Is Niki laughing?

"Not yet."

"You will. Are you coming to school today? Everybody's talking about the game."

"Maybe not."

"Modest guy. Okay. See you tomorrow. Bye."

By two o'clock Booger is back to normal size. His outer skin still has some blotchy, scabby patches but even they are disappearing with a speed that astonishes JW who is used to seeing animals with burns at *The Pet Vet*. He puts Booger in the swing beside Mick and calls Sheriff Riley on the cordless. He isn't letting Booger out of his sight. Ever.

"Hi Sheriff Riley, it's JW. I've had my bike stolen... no, not that one. It was my dad's brand new bike but I was riding it. I was hoping you could tell me where most stolen bikes turn up?"

The answer to this question turns out to be the answer to a lot of questions: McDonalds, Wendy's, Burger King, Crummie's. In other words Fast Food and Stolen Bikes go together like hamburgers and French fries.

JW forms a picture of a bicycle in his brain and before you can say "Crummie Burgers are the best" Booger is beside him a bicycle in black. Shiny like a bowling ball.

"Are you sure you're okay?"

Booger's answer to this is to start down the driveway without JW.

"Okay yourself. We're going hunting for my dad's bike. This is the third time I've lost his bike so it would be *really good* to find it before he misses it."

JW does not start by following Sheriff Riley's advice but rides over to Granite High instead. He wants to check the bike rack there to make sure the thief hasn't ridden the bike to school. Riding the bike to school would be mucho dumb but JW figures anybody who'd steal a bike in the first place probably has an IQ that matches his shoe size.

His dad's bike isn't at Granite. Or McDonalds. Or Booger King (Booger's idea.). Or Wendy's. Or Pizza Hut.

But it is at Crummie's. Under the big neon hamburger sign. The one where the bun opens and the patty falls out. The one that says "Over 17 sold."

So is his dad. So is Yummy with Amanda. So is Niki. So is Gloria with Dougie. So is Jack Granite in his black Mercedes sports car.

"You must be feeling better," his dad says making room for JW at the picnic table.

"Would you like something, JW?" asks Yummy.

Before JW can answer Niki appears at his elbow with a chocolate milkshake. JW introduces Niki to his dad.

"How's Eddie doing?" Niki asks.

Amanda beams. "He can come home next week."

The conversation wanders in circles for some minutes until Dr. Martin stands up to leave.

"Back to work. Whose bike is that, JW?"

"The black one? Uh, that would be... Niki's bike."

"Nice. See you later. Bye everyone."

JW watches his dad go. Yummy heads off with Amanda but is immediately corralled by Jack Granite. JW tries his Vulcan Mind Control again. It's never worked but there has to be a first time.

Don't sell Yummy — Don't sell Yummy — Don't sell...

"So, I like my new bike," Niki says.

JW grins. "Thought you might. Wanna ride it home?"

"What about my other bike?"

"That old thing. Hmmmm. Age-old problem of three bikes and two riders, much more difficult than two bikes and three riders. Hmmmm. Go get bike. Wise man make three an' two add up four."

By the time Niki gets back with her bike the shiny black bike is gone and JW is wearing a lime-green backpack.

Niki, on the other hand, is wearing a *Startled Look of Disbelief*. It's blush-red, has wide eyes and looks good on her.

"It wasn't a story!"

The Plot Thickens

Jack Granite is EXASPERATED. And SCARED. The last time those two happened together he'd been running out of oxygen and trying to open an airlock on the Lunar Module that didn't want to open. This isn't much different.

"Yummy, listen to me. Six million for Crummie's is at least triple what it's worth," he says smiling the Jack Granite, former astronaut, richest guy in town, neon smile. The one with the Dazzling White Teeth.

"Jack," Yummy says smiling back. "It's worth whatever you'll pay for it and one dollar more."

"Yeah, Sal, I like it." Mark Nash is sitting at his desk doodling on his green blotter. Sal's been talking for ten minutes about Shipstead and Dr. Martin's place and all the weird animals that live there. Mark Nash can see Cynthia through the window getting ready to dive into the swimming pool. At least you can't cry underwater.

"Yeah, yeah, it's positive, I like that. We'll keep the other idea as back-up. Would you ask him first?... but if he says 'no' the whole thing's kaput. If we don't ask him, just announce it, he'll have to go along, right? I bet he'll love the idea. All that travel, helping animals... let's do it... yeah, this weekend. I'm running out of time here."

&

"I'm telling you he bought a cake mix and a thing of icing and as he was leaving he waved to me. AND, he was smiling."

Ernest "Don't Call Me Ernie" Brown is pacing back and forth in his brother Douglas' bedroom. His brother is the only boy he knows with a tidy room. Dougie is watching him, thinking. He's thinking his butt still hurts from that dumb toilet.

"Did you e-mail Uncle Peter?" Ernie asks.

"Yeah, I told him I really liked the Milky Way in a Coke Bottle he sent last year and has he seen anything that nifty this year?"

"And?"

"And he hasn't gotten back to me."

Dougie's butt hurts but not as much as his pride. It looks like the No-Water Toilet is No-More. But Dougie isn't giving up on winning Inventors without a fight.

"That bike JW's invented sounds good," Dougie says. His friend Squeaky Cotter happened to be looking out his window the night JW had to demonstrate his bike to Sheriff Riley. He told Douglas all about it. "Man, you should have seen the wheels on JW's bike changing sizes. It was like some kind of buckin' bronco ride, JW hangin' on for dear life."

"Squeaky says it's good enough to win Inventors."

Ernie stops. He puts his left hand to his ear. He puts his right hand straight up in the air, index finger extended.

"Are you on *before* JW?"

"I'm second last, he's last."

Ernie grins. "IDEA! INCOMING!"

Roman passes the phone to Jack Granite. His hand is shaking.

"No. Not yet," Jack Granite says into the phone. He listens some more. "Yes Max, I know this is taking too long."

Jack Granite is staring out his living room window at the ocean.

All of a sudden two men appear in his backyard. He knows them —
Hans and Joe — tough guys. They work for Max Keefer, the man on
the phone. Jack Granite watches as Hans, the younger of the two
men, throws the ball for Mantis. Mantis runs back to Hans and drops
the ball at his feet.

"Yes Max, I know Afghans are a very old breed. Sighthounds.
Fast enough to hunt gazelle and snow leopards."

Jack stares as Hans holds the ball up. Mantis gets up on his hind
legs and walks after the ball.

"No, I didn't know they could walk like that... so they can see
the game in tall grass, interesting."

Now Hans has a gun in his hand.

"Max, no, please. You don't need..." Hans pulls the trigger. Jack
winces as the ball in Mantis' mouth explodes. Mantis runs off. Joe
and Hans leave but not before Hans waves goodbye.

"Yes, I know what will happen if I don't resolve this."

Jack Granite hands the phone back to Roman. His whole body is
shaking. How did he ever get into this mess? And more important,
how is he ever going to get out of it?

Every Other Friday

JW hates Every Other Friday. It means he has to say goodbye to his friends and go to Mark Nash's place in San Francisco.

In the beginning, Dr. Martin drove the kids halfway to a service station on the PCH where JW's mother would pick them up. Sunday night went the other way. But these meetings proved to be too painful for everyone so Mark Nash, Famous Rock Star and Rotten Person spoke up.

"Darlin', why don't I send a car and driver and we'll let somebody else do all the driving?"

This seemed like a good idea until the car Mark Nash sent turned out to be his stretch limousine that was so stretched it could barely turn a corner without backing up. And it wasn't white and it wasn't black like normal stretch limos, it was gold. The license plate read MARKNASH, just so there'd be no doubt as to who owned this totally useless car that got three hundred feet to the gallon.

At first it was exciting sitting in the back of the limo watching Mark Nash videos, eating snacks from the drawer in the coffee table that opened automatically when you pushed the snack button on the remote, drinking pop from the mini-bar, talking to mom on the video phone.

But JW couldn't forget the look on his dad's face as the limo drove away.

Words like *goodness* and *kindness* and loneliness are hard to capture in your mind's eye but JW knew what *sadness* looked like.

It looked like his dad waving goodbye.

There weren't any limousines after that. JW told his mom if she wanted him to come to San Francisco Mark Nash better send a car that didn't look like it belonged at Fort Knox. The twins couldn't understand what his problem was but JW knew they were uncomfortable too.

One ride in a limo was fun. Two rides was... ostentatious was the word JW wanted but he didn't know it. It means the act of displaying vainly or pretentiously in order to excite admiration. In other words, Look At Me, I Have More Money Than You. Aren't I Great!

Mark Nash's penthouse on Pacific Avenue was ostentatious too but at least it wasn't driving around pointing at itself. It was on the top floor of the Nash Building, in fact it was the top floor.

It had six bedrooms, seven bathrooms, a living room so big if you came in from the kitchen eating a hotdog, the hotdog would be gone before you made it to the thirty-foot leather couch. The TV was flat plasma running from floor to ceiling. On Sunday afternoon the San Francisco 49ers were bigger on Mark Nash's wall than they were in real life. Between the kitchen and the living room was a wall-to-ceiling salt-water aquarium filled with brightly colored tropical fish including a baby manta ray.

The outside balcony was wide enough to have a full-sized swimming pool with a rock waterfall surrounded by jungle garden and one end wall of the pool was made of glass behind which was a television screen playing computer-generated graphics. The whole place overlooked San Francisco Bay and the Golden Gate Bridge. At night with all the lights on the view alone was worth millions.

And try as he might not to like Mark Nash and his STUFF even JW had to admit the weight room, the recording studio and the room full of antique pinball machines were actually pretty cool.

But even surrounded by all these neat things JW never feels at home here. He feels like the third guy in a two-man tent or a little kid at a grown-up party. He sometimes wonders if his mom feels like a visitor here too. They don't talk about those kinds of things. She asks him about school and his dad and the clinic. JW doesn't ask questions. There's nothing he wants to know about.

Georgia and Paula are better with the whole thing. They talk to their mom all weekend and go shopping and get their hair done and they like the attention that spills over onto them when they're out with Mark Nash. JW has to admit Mark Nash is good to all three kids and certainly treats their mom with respect. There's just something about Mark Nash that doesn't work for JW. Maybe he'll figure it out this weekend.

Rick usually drives the car but today it's Juan. He reminds JW of Inigo Montoya from the *Princess Bride*.

"So Juanboy," Juan says. "Wat you dink dat *WaterWorld*? I go last week, thirst time I eber been. Nice place but wet, y'know? Five minutes you soaked, right? I take Maria, nice girl but not toooo nice, y'know? We walk in gate we soaked. T-shirts soaked. Berry nice, y'know what I mean? Girls and wet t-shirts dis ees a good ding. Right Pwala, you agree, right? Girls and water good ding."

Juan looks back at the road ahead.

"I tell you one more ding. You go *WaterWorld* don't buy popcorn."

They've had Juan before. He talks the whole way which is okay because he's funny but unfortunately Juan can't speak unless he's looking at the person he's talking to. To talk to Paula, who's sitting behind him, Juan has to turn practically around which would be okay if he wasn't driving.

"Look out, look out. Neber hab I seen such bad drivers as here in 'Nited Tates. In Meheeco we get five, sex cars in road dis size, here two an they drive like road belong to dem. I tinkin' I might open scule. Teech ebyone to drybe like Juan."

JW tries to imagine everyone *drybing* like Juan.

Maybe all the cars could be made out of rubber?

Georgia has a suggestion. "Hey Juan, rather than turn around why don't you use the rearview mirror?"

Juan grabs hold of the rearview mirror and tilts it till he can see Georgia.

"Dis ees what you speakin' about?" Georgia nods. "Dis ees not for looking, dis ees for puttin on liptick, combin de hair, checkin de teeth. You too young know dis but someday, y'know? Hey Pwalla, don't talk much today. I tink dis ees because you tink I may have unger brudder who ees better looking than me so why waste time wit Juan, right? But how ees dis possible, I can hear myself ask dis? How dis be possible? No one better lookin' than Juan."

It occurs to JW that if Juan is going to talk to Paula the whole way they would be better off driving backwards.

"Hey, JW. Where'd you get the new gym bag?"

Paula is leaning forward looking for something behind her and in the process has noticed JW's new gym bag which is sitting beside him on the front seat. It's a Nike bag, silver with black stripes. Guess who?

"I borrowed it from Niki."

"You like Niki," Paula says smiling a girl smile.

"I thought your motto was no girl over two blocks UP," says Georgia. Juan perks up.

"Wat is dis no girl to block up? Juanboy please, dis is sumding I should be knowin' bout, right?"

JW looks at Juan. There's just nowhere to start. He looks back at Georgia.

"My new motto is never talk to twin sisters in a moving vehicle."

"Ha, ha, dis ees good. I need dis rule wit my sister. I tell her 'yur mouth ess bigger than yur butt.'"

Georgia leans forward.

"Just for the record we never *liked* Gloria."

"Too *girly*," Paula says.

Whatever that means.

They make it to San Francisco. Juan doesn't take them to the penthouse but drops them off at a restaurant called *Uppity's*. JW and the twins go inside to be greeted by a black marble foyer and a chandelier as big as a car.

JW makes a face. Mark Nash is always doing this to them. They're dressed in their jeans, JW has a black Harley Davidson t-shirt on, Paula is wearing an American flag sweater and Georgia an orange tank top that says *Fried Green Tomatoes* that she got in Georgia last summer.

And they're carrying their bags.

Everybody they can see in the dining room is dressed like they're auditioning for President of the United States. There are enough pearls to make a harbor and enough shiny black shoes to make a stealth bomber.

"Forget this. Let's get a cab." But before JW can turn around he hears his mom's voice behind him.

"There you are. I was afraid you'd have to wait." Cynthia kisses her three children in turn. She's wearing a short black dress and not pearls but diamonds. Her dark hair is cut short. Her diamond earrings sparkle just like the chandelier

Paula is the first to speak. "Mom, you look *so hot.*"

Cynthia laughs. "C'mon, we are going to set this place on fire!"

They don't go into the restaurant they go to a room off to the side. There, waiting for them, are boxes of clothes. Black dresses for the girls with diamond necklaces and earrings. Black high heels. Cynthia hands JW a tuxedo and a pair of those black shiny shoes he loves so much and points to the men's washroom.

JW studies himself in the mirror. He never thinks of himself as handsome but for a second he sees himself running up on stage to accept his Oscar. Then he sees himself returning to his seat and getting a big hug and kiss from Niki.

But as good as JW looks he's pale compared to the twins. They're sensational. Their blond hair and dark tans combined with the simple black dresses and the diamonds lead to only one word, WOW!

And if you look at that word WOW! the W's could be Paula and Georgia and the O could be JW and the exclamation mark ! could be... that's right, The Kid from the Hot Tub, because Booger is no longer a silver Nike gym bag. He's supposed to be an elegant walking stick — you know shiny black with a silver knob, the kind you dance with if you're in an old movie and know how to tap dance — but he's not.

Of course, the problem was JW didn't have anything to show Booger so all he could do was make a picture in his brain and hope for the best.

Of course, there were transmission difficulties. Telepathy is not an exact science like mathematics or chemistry; it's more like chicken sexing or throwing knuckleballs.

Who knows what might happen?

Booger's first attempt at a walking stick looked remarkably like the hockey stick Mick has in his cage. JW was tempted to go with this but it was hard to see exactly how a hockey stick fitted in with a tuxedo.

Try again Boog.

Booger tried again and this time got the shape right but the consistency was wrong. It looked like JW was carrying a dead snake.

Once more.

Booger's third attempt was spectacular. He got everything right but the length. The walking stick shot up through the ceiling into the washroom above piercing a hole in the toilet directly over JW's head.

JW looked up to see a wave of water coming his way but just before it hit Booger changed into a black umbrella and the day was saved.

Sort of.

୬

Even JW has to admit, as a group, they are impressive. His mom looks like a million bucks and his two sisters aren't far behind. How the girls know how to walk in high heels is another of *life's little mysteries*. If JW tried it he'd break both ankles at the same time. He figures it must be hereditary.

But the person who makes it all work has to be Mark Nash, Famous Rock Star and Rotten Person. Like JW he has on a tux but there is a difference. As good as JW looks he still looks like he's wearing a Halloween costume. But Mark Nash — tall, blond, slim, rugged — looks like the original tuxedo was made especially for him.

JW has a brief flash of Mark Nash as a one-year-old wearing a tuxedo and a diaper. The black umbrella in his hand spins around once and JW laughs with Booger. There's no point fighting any of this so JW makes up his mind to enjoy it. Mark Nash leads the way into the dining room his flotilla following behind him.

To say they cause a stir would be like saying the Super Bowl is just another football game. The restaurant stops.

Nothing moves but eyes and heads. Forks hang suspended in mid-air. Waiters, who have seen everything three times, stand frozen balancing four plates and the mayor's wife's fifth glass of wine. All of a sudden you can hear the piano playing. It's something. JW's umbrella vibrates in his hand.

"I feel like Princess Di," Georgia says trying to whisper in the silence.

"She's dead," whispers back Paula.

"You know what I mean!"

They are seated in a round booth just to the right of the stage. On stage is a young black woman at a grand piano playing something old that JW doesn't recognize. She smiles at Mark Nash and keeps playing. If there is a menu JW never sees it but that doesn't stop food from appearing. Niki keeps popping up in his brain. She would so love this.

JW has a brief flash of Gloria but that's followed by a dose of Dougie. They melt into a giant crab and disappear. Booger keeps sending pictures of baby Mark Nash in various ridiculous outfits. Right now he's a rubber ducky wearing a diaper. *Enough Booger* sends JW in danger of laughing out loud for no apparent reason.

Everything that is put in front of JW is his favorite. Shrimp cocktail, Caesar salad with a hundred toasted croutons, ribs with hot barbeque sauce, baked potato with the inside whipped, topped with butter and fresh sour cream, chocolate mousse dribbled with caramel sauce and deep-purple berries that JW doesn't recognize but that melt in his mouth.

And feeding Booger is easy. JW just drops stuff into his umbrella.

His mom looks happy. She's beside Mark Nash and he has his arm around her bare shoulders. They're drinking coffee and Mark Nash has an unlit cigar in his mouth. The piano player finishes her song and there is polite applause. She pulls the microphone closer.

"Thank you. Now that Mark Nash has finished his dinner I was hoping we might convince him to come up here and sing a song for us."

There is more applause, some whistles, words of encouragement. Mark Nash stands up, waves, kisses Cynthia, winks at the Twins.

While everybody is busy watching Mark Nash, Famous Rock Star and Rotten Person, JW scrapes the rest of his chocolate mousse into his umbrella. Paula hasn't touched hers. JW nudges her arm and she passes it over to him. Paula has stars in her eyes.

JW hopes Booger likes chocolate. Too late it occurs to him that you aren't supposed to feed chocolate to animals. It isn't good for them. Makes them sick.

Is Booger an animal?

Oh boy, better not think about that, thinks JW. Booger might be listening.

Mark Nash takes the microphone, stands beside the piano.

"Let's try an old Beatles song, *All I've Got to Do* and then I have two important announcements I would like to make." The piano player begins to play and Mark Nash looks over at Cynthia.

And when I want to kiss you,
All I've got to do,
Is whisper in your ear,
The words you long to hear,
And I'll be kissing you...

All night JW has been forced to reconsider his aversion to Mark Nash, Famous Rock Star and Maybe Not Rotten Person. But there is still something crawling around, JW just can't put his finger on it.

It's the same feeling he has when he thinks about Jack Granite buying Crummie's.

And take this song. It's one of his mom's favorites but he's never heard it sung like this, slower with only a piano in the background. He knows Mark Nash can sing but now he knows Mark Nash can *really* sing.

But he also knows none of this just happened. It's all a set-up.

Mark Nash and the piano player have probably practiced this song for hours.

Waiter, there's a snake in my soup.

"Thank you." Mark Nash makes Marcia, the pianist, take a bow. "Now if I could have a few minutes of your time I would like to introduce my *family* to you."

JW stares at Mark Nash, startled. There's a phrase, *like a deer in the headlights,* and that's the look that's all over JW's face. *Family?* Suddenly he's scared. Something bad is happening here.

"First, I'd like you to meet my best friend, Cynthia Martin." Mark Nash makes Cynthia join him on stage. People clap. Some of the men whistle.

"And this is her son, John, better known as JW."

JW is glued to his chair. It's going to take a crane to pull him out of this seat.

"JW?"

It's his mom's voice. There is a look on her face that says *please JW, for me.* JW stands up and walks on stage. He's squeezing the umbrella so hard he knows he's probably hurting Booger but he can't stop. The applause dies down.

"And Cynthia's daughters, Georgia and Paula." It's as the twins are heading for the stage that JW realizes there are photographers coming towards them and he can see at least two men at the back with headphones and television cameras with blinking red lights.

They're now standing in a line on stage with Mark Nash in the middle the twins at either end.

"My first announcement is this, Cynthia and I are engaged to be married."

Oh man, don't do this. JW is the deer in the headlights and the headlights belong to a transport truck.

"Thank you... thank you... My second announcement is Cynthia and I have decided to start The Mark Nash Foundation for the Preservation of Rare and Endangered Animals. This is a subject that all of us here on stage feel very strongly about."

Right, thinks JW. The only animals Mark Nash has ever mentioned are the Miami *Dolphins* and the Chicago *Bears*.

People are on their feet now, clapping, whistling. JW stands frozen waiting for impact.

"And, it is with pride that I announce that Cynthia's former husband, Dr. George Martin of Shipstead, California will head our new foundation."

Mark Nash has another paragraph to go outlining how Dr. Martin will travel the world spending the $10 million dollars that Mark Nash is giving to the Foundation but he never gets any of these words out because at the same time as Cynthia turns to say, "You never told me that!" JW, in one motion, swings his umbrella up and opens it so that the photographers will get nothing more than a photo of a big black circle.

But, as usual these days, nothing would be complete without Booger playing his part and this time Booger's part is over-the-top, the *crème de la crème*, as they say in the kitchen. Here's what happens.

Poor Booger hasn't eaten any of the food that JW has been depositing in his umbrella because he's been afraid he might, *starts with f rhymes with heart*, or *WORSE*. These are things Booger and JW discussed before leaving for the city so they're fresh in Booger's mind.

As a result, when JW flings open the umbrella, Booger — not wanting Mommy to see he hasn't eaten any of the nice food — tries to hide the evidence by exploding like a shotgun pelting everybody on stage with shrimps, lettuce, croutons, rib bones, baked potato, sour cream and chocolate mousse. This barrage creams everybody but especially Mark Nash, Famous Rock Star and Potential Landfill Site.

12

Swimming Under the Stars

Georgia, Paula and Cynthia are sitting in the back of the limo still wearing their daring black dresses and darling diamond earrings. JW has changed back into his street clothes. He's sitting facing the females. Booger is a backpack lying at JW's feet. Mark Nash isn't in the limo at all. He's walking home so he can cool down on the way.

"I'm sorry," JW's mom says. "I think he meant well."

JW doesn't say anything. Everybody in the limo is angry but for different reasons.

"We looked wonderful till you opened that *stupid* umbrella," Georgia says.

"Why did you put food in it?" Paula wants to know.

"I thought you both looked good in chocolate."

"It's not funny!"

"That part *was* funny. Bringing Dad into it wasn't funny. That part was mean."

"Enough JW." Cynthia isn't the kind to get angry but she's angry now, mostly at Mark Nash and some because what should have been a wonderful evening has turned out to be the opposite. When they arrive at the penthouse JW goes to the pinball room and takes out his frustration on King Kong. Finally he thinks to phone his dad but when he picks up the phone he hears a still pissed-off Mark Nash talking to someone named Sal.

"How do I know why there was food in the friggin' umbrella. Why was there an umbrella in the first place is more to the point. And there's no way I'm putting ten million into saving warthogs in Borneo!"

Booger isn't angry. He's hungry. After everyone has gone to bed, JW takes him to the kitchen disguised as a four-foot-high potted palm. Booger eats enough food for three teenagers.

"JW?"

"Hi mom."

"I'm sorry I lost my temper."

"That's okay. It wasn't your fault."

"Who are you talking to?"

"This potted palm."

"Oh, that's good. They say plants grow better if you talk to them. I don't suppose you'd like to go for a swim? It's a nice night and I can't sleep."

"I'd love to. Is it okay if I bring my friend?"

"Friends are always welcome."

It *is* a nice night out. Black with millions of stars. The water is warm and the pool has dim underwater lights that make you feel like you're swimming in phosphorus. JW's mom is a beautiful swimmer and slips effortlessly through the water. JW makes more noise but he gets the job done.

"What's that?" Cynthia asks watching a dolphin-like creature glide through the water. JW looks over where the potted palm should be but isn't.

Booger, Booger, Booger.

Yes, Mommy?

"That would be my Alien Being," JW answers.

"Funny boy. It's probably some new toy of Mark's. Whatever it is it's certainly at home in the water."

JW looks at his mother as if she has just solved one of *life's little mysteries*.

"Boog?"

Yes Mommy?

"You see all those stars up there?"

JW is sitting on a deck chair beside the pool staring up at the stars. His mom has gone to bed. Booger the Jellybean is sitting in the chair beside him. Suddenly JW sees a ball of light coming out of the night sky hurtling towards him like a runaway comet. JW manages to jump to his feet but that's all. The comet crashes into his stomach throwing him backwards into the pool.

JW's brain fills with laughter.

Booger!

Yes Mommy?

JW wants to scold Booger but for what? Having fun?

That was funny Booger. You like it in the water, don't you?

JW's brain fills with happiness. JW comes up for air. Booger the Dolphin pops up beside him.

"Boog, do you know where you're from?"

Booger shakes his head.

"Wherever it is I bet there's a lot of water."

It suddenly occurs to JW that maybe Booger is from Earth but way in the future. Or maybe from some parallel universe where there aren't human beings but Boogers instead.

"Okay, let's play a game. I'll think of something and you try to become that."

JW shuts his eyes and pictures an Orca, a killer whale. Booger turns into a Sardine with Spoiler. JW can see getting the size right is tricky. JW tries again. This time he pictures the whale with a man standing beside it. Booger does much better this time except Booger is so big half the Orca is out of the pool. *If someone comes now, thinks JW.*

"Stay in the pool, Boog."

Booger shrinks, the Orca drops into the pool with a splash and opens its mouth.

And swallows JW.

After that JW is content to let Booger make his own shapes like Giant Spider Walking Upside Down on Surface of Pool, Water Snake with Head at Each End, Squid Meeting Octopus, Manta Ray Flying In and Out of Water. Then JW makes the mistake of wishing Niki was there to share this beautiful evening and suddenly she is there in a tiny black bathing suit her long black hair streaming out behind her.

"No way Boog! That's just too weird."

Booger morphs into a mermaid with long red hair, the same pretty mermaid that's on the label of the Twins' shampoo.

"I just wish the *real* Niki was here. And I wish it wasn't too late to call her."

JW can feel Booger sending him a message. It feels like *send her a message.*

Niki I wish you were here, sends JW grinning. His first Cosmic Postcard.

By the next morning Mark Nash, Famous Rock Star and Confirmed Rotten Person has calmed down.

"Look at this picture. I look like I'm wearing an eyepatch. Not bad. I might try that at my next concert. A new look. Mark Nash, Pirate." He holds the newspaper up so JW can see what he's talking about. It still looks like chocolate mousse to JW but he doesn't say anything.

"And JW, I got to ask you. Where did that umbrella come from and why in tarnation was it full of food?"

JW looks down at the potted palm at his feet and smiles. He's getting the hang of things, just like Booger.

"Actually, if you want to know, I've created an Alien Being in my hot tub at home and this Alien Being can take any shape he wants and at the moment he's this potted palm tree." JW holds up the palm tree then pours his bowl of Honey Nut Cheerios into it. "But last night he was an umbrella and I was putting food in the umbrella so he wouldn't starve to death."

Mark Nash shakes his head. Like all big stars Mark Nash controls most of the people around him. He pays them, they do what he says. Those he doesn't control are usually in awe of him which amounts to pretty much the same thing. He isn't used to someone who doesn't like him and Cynthia's JW fits into that category. And the fiasco last night has just made matters worse.

But Mark Nash, Famous Rock Star and Rotten Person, knows that "he who fights and runs away, may live to fight another day." There will definitely be another day and that day will be *soon*.

13

Dumb Debbie

It's Sunday morning in Shipstead. Dougie watches as Dr. Martin and his three-legged dog get into the red Jeep Cherokee and drive away. Dougie knows JW and his sisters are at their mother's in San Francisco. Gloria told him. Having Gloria mad at JW is helping a lot, plus she's pretending to be Dougie's girlfriend — she says to make JW jealous — but Dougie doesn't care.

He's never had a girlfriend before, well, that isn't exactly true. Martha Sharpe liked him in second grade till she got her glasses.

"Oh," she said bringing Dougie into focus for the first time. "I thought you were wearing swimming goggles or something. Yuck."

Dougie couldn't figure out why a kid would be wearing swimming goggles to school but it was obviously something Martha thought was okay. The next day Dougie did wear swimming goggles.

"Too late," Martha said. "Still yuck."

That's the way it had been for Dougie with girls ever since. Yuck and more yuck. So having a pretty girl like Gloria acting like his girlfriend is a new experience for Dougie and one that he is enjoying. That's why it's so important for him to win Inventors again. He has to show Gloria that being handsome on the outside is nothing to being handsome within.

Dougie reaches into his pocket and pulls out an iPhone, the one he's borrowed from his mom's purse, the one he isn't allowed to use EVER, because he'd once called his friend Ralph in England. Ralph had moved there from Shipstead and after they'd talked Dougie had forgotten to push the *off* button. The bill, when it came, made his mom fall down.

$4,324.17

"We could have all flown there for that, you rotten bonehead!" she cried between sobs.

Fortunately, the phone company forgave all but a hundred dollars which Dougie had to pay out of his own money. But Dougie wasn't sure his mom would ever forgive him.

"I had too much fun when I was young," she'd say. "And now I'm being punished."

But winning Inventors two years in a row might change that as well. Dougie punches in a number.

"Whole Foods, Debbie speaking. How may I help you?"

Oh no, Dumb Debbie. Dougie crosses his fingers.

"Hi Debbie, it's Douglas Brown. Is Ernest there?"

"Of course, he's here. Where else would he be?"

"Could I speak to him please?"

"You know we're not supposed to take personal calls."

Dougie makes a face. He might be a nerd but at least he has a brain. Debbie is so far from the sharpest knife in the drawer she's not even in the drawer.

"It's an emergency."

"Oh yeah, right. Like I can hear sirens in the background."

"No really, mom's fallen in the bathtub, please get Ernest."

"I'll tell him." The line goes dead. Dougie shuts his eyes. The world's simplest plan defeated by the world's dumbest person. How fair is that?

Dougie redials.

"Whole Foods, Mike-the-Manager speaking. How may I help you?"

This time it's Dougie who hangs up.

Dougie strolls up the Martin's driveway like he belongs there. Just visiting my good friend JW, don't you know? He tries the side door of the garage. It pops open. He peers inside. Mick, the gorilla, is looking at him. Good thing there's a cage.

Dougie comes inside letting his eyes adjust to the light. He looks around. This seems like the logical place to find JW's magic bike unless JW has hidden it, of course. Dougie would have hidden it if it had been his magic bike but he isn't sure JW thinks like he does. In fact, he's pretty sure JW doesn't think like he does because Dougie has never met *anybody* who thinks like he does. But it was probably the same for Einstein, thinks Dougie, proving his point.

"So, Mr. Gorilla, do you know where JW's magic bike is?"

When Dougie is nervous he talks to himself. He walks through the three bays of the garage. He finds the girls' bikes and JW's normal bike, the one with the bent front wheel, but that's it. He climbs the stairs. JW's dumb parrot is there and a big red bird with a long bill.

Dougie looks up the dead tree sticking through the roof. The three-toed sloth is at the top, sleeping by the looks of things. In all the times Dougie has ridden by JW's house he's never seen the sloth move but it's never in the same place either so it must move once in awhile.

"Probably right up there with watching paint dry," Dougie says. He's heard people laugh at this so he chuckles.

"Nine One One!" squawks Janis Joplin. Dougie's heart hits the roof and bounces back down. Dougie stares at the parrot. He can't see a cell phone anywhere and her feathers aren't bulging. He decides she must be bluffing.

"You're bluffing."

"You have the right to remain silent," Janis squawks. "Anything you say…"

Dougie hurries downstairs. The gorilla is in his cage riding a bicycle. It's Dr. Martin's bicycle but Dougie doesn't know that. His knees turn to jelly. Oh no, please, anything but that.

Dougie studies Mick through the bars. It looks like a normal bike he's riding. The wheels are the same size.

"That can't be it," Dougie says.

The back door of the house isn't locked. Dougie steps inside and listens. The house is quiet.

"Can it be breaking and entering when you don't break anything?"

There isn't anyone to answer Dougie but he's pretty sure he knows the answer to his question. He walks through the kitchen into the backroom. He's been to JW's house before with his mom. Someone had organized a tour of Shipstead's mansions to raise money for something. He remembers the big snake in the backroom. And there it is in its cage eyeing him like he might just eat Dougie for lunch if something better doesn't come along.

Dougie remembers asking his mom how she'd like to live with a big snake like that in her house?

"Can't be any worse than living with two nincompoops," she'd answered. Dougie sighs. It's a good thing he likes being a nerd or his self-esteem would be in the dumpster.

There is no bike that Dougie can see. The snake flicks its tongue at him.

"Real tough guy with the cage to protect you," Dougie says.

Dougie heads upstairs looking for JW's room. It isn't hard to find. Everything JW owns is either on the walls or on the floor. It's an even bigger mess than his brother Ernest's room, the room that his mother says looks like a dump after a nuclear explosion. Dougie stands in the doorway. Despite the piles of stuff everywhere there isn't a mound big enough to hide a bicycle. And it isn't under the bed though everything else is.

Dougie makes a path to JW's walk-in closet. On the door is a poster of John Lennon and running down the side are the words to *Imagine*.

Dougie opens the door.

This is *A Big Mistake*.

When Dougie wakes up he's surrounded by white. Either his glasses are bent out of shape or his eyeballs are moving in concentric circles. Whatever's happening Dougie is having trouble focusing.

"I can't be dead, my head hurts too much for that," Dougie says, the words bouncing off the tiled walls. His hand is reaching around for his mom's iPhone, the one he is never to touch for as long as he lives. It isn't that big a room he's in but his hand isn't finding anything but cool white tiles, the kind you would find in a bathroom.

Dougie straightens his glasses and sits up. That hurts. He looks around. He is in a bathroom. The walls are covered in photographs of the Beatles. Definitely JW's house. He stands up. That hurts too.

There's a window. If he stands on the toilet he can look out. He's still on the second floor. Dougie can see a wooden deck below him with a hot tub and off to the side he can see something big moving around in the backyard. It's some kind of lizard. A big one. If you were buying it a t-shirt you'd buy XXXL.

Dougie wobbles to the door and tries the handle. Locked.

"How can you lock a bathroom door from the outside?" asks Dougie. No one answers. If JW had been there he might have told Dougie he changed the door handles so that he could lock Booger in the bathroom if he had to. In case of emergencies.

Dougie rattles the doorknob. Something is moving around on the other side of the door. Probably that stupid blue-butted baboon. The one that surprised Dougie in the walk-in closet. The one that hit him on the head with a golf club. Dougie touches his forehead. He has a lump like a golf ball.

"Figures," Dougie says.

What's the baboon's name? Eric Something.

"Eric, let me out of here!" Dougie shouts but wishes he hadn't. The words are like knives flying around in his head. He waits but nothing happens. He goes back to the window. It opens and is big enough to crawl out of. Dougie looks down. There is nothing to stand on. It's straight down to the deck about sixteen feet. He looks up. The roof hangs over and there is a gutter but he'll never reach it. Where is Spiderman when you need him?

Dougie searches the room for the iPhone. His plan had been to phone Ernest at work, tell him he was going into JW's house to find the magic bike and if Dougie didn't phone back in ten minutes, Ernest was to come and rescue him. But Dumb Debbie wrecked that plan like rain at a weenie roast.

No iPhone.

If he doesn't find it his mother will ground him till he's dead and buried.

Maybe longer.

Dougie crouches on the window ledge. The hot tub is below him about six feet out from the wall and three feet over. Dougie has seen a man on TV jump off a little platform and land in a pool of water no bigger than the hot tub. And the man had been much higher up, but the pool he dove into had been deeper. And the man was coordinated.

Dougie isn't coordinated. He's a nerd. Coordinated people, like athletes, can jump off a window ledge and aim where they are going to land. Like in the middle of a hot tub. Nerds jump off hoping the hot tub will move to wherever they are going to land.

"Please don't let me be a rim shot," Dougie says. He sends the signal from his brain to his legs to jump but his brain and his legs know he doesn't really mean it. He's not ready they say.

"I'm going to count to three and then jump." The XXX-L Lizard in the backyard stares up at him. The lizard yawns.

"One… two… two-and-a-half… two-and-three-quarters…"

Dougie stops. He can hear a scraping noise. He watches as the blue-butted baboon pulls a director's chair up to the hot tub and sits down. The baboon looks up at Dougie and grins. Then he holds up Dougie's iPhone and wiggles it.

"I can't believe this," Dougie says. He is going to die and the only witnesses are going to be an XXX-L Lizard, yawning, and a stupid, blue-butted baboon, grinning.

His mother was always saying *Life Isn't Fair* and she was usually looking at Douglas and Ernest when she said it, but this is beyond that. This is like a blizzard at a weenie roast.

Dougie watches as the blue-butted baboon puts his paw in the air. Then he watches as the paw opens and ONE digit pops up. Then TWO. Then THREE.

Dougie jumps.

Manfred holds the little silver box while Mann pushes the buttons. It is really very nice of Eric to bring them their very first mobile phone. They aren't exactly sure what you do with it but they like the noises it makes when you push the buttons.

All at once there is a ringing noise and then a man is speaking to them. "G'day mate. You've reached the World Weather info line, a service of the Australian Meteorological Bureau and Quantas Airlines. The temperature today in Buenos Aires…"

Manfred smiles. This is nice. They can listen to the weather around the world and pretend to be in each country. Kind of like an all-you-can-eat buffet of sun, clouds, showers, hurricanes and typhoons.

Manfred closes his eye. Best of all he can have a short snooze.

"Mann?"

"Yes, Manfred?"

"Wake me when we get to Zimbabwe."

When Dougie finally arrives home, leaving a trail of wet behind him like a giant slug, a police car and an ambulance are parked in the driveway, their lights flashing. Mrs. Latchford, his neighbor, is standing on the sidewalk brushing her hair.

"Oh Douglas, there you are. Your mother is looking for you. Your brother came running home shouting your mother had fallen in the bathtub but I don't think that can be true because she looked dry standing in the doorway screaming your name. Oh, you're the one that's all wet. Have you had an accident dear? Why don't you come inside for a moment and we'll tidy you up. I don't think your mom would want to see you like that. In fact, I'm not sure she wants to see you at all."

Dougie follows Mrs. Latchford into her house. Maybe he could live with the Latchfords till he's old enough to leave home.

"Lloyd?"

"Yes, dear?"

"Douglas is here."

"I'm going to your mother's. Phone me when he's gone."

Maybe not.

14

Hope Springs Eternal

JW and the twins arrive back at Grove Street about two o'clock on Sunday afternoon. Things weren't *right* at the penthouse and when JW asked his mom if they could go home early she didn't argue with him. Their dad isn't home. JW is worried about him so he punches in his dad's cell number and hits speakerphone so the twins can hear.

"Dad? Where are you?"

"I'm on the beach at Port Reyes. Yummy and Amanda are here with me. Where are you?"

"We're home early. No one wanted to stay after last night."

"I had reporters calling all morning. I told them I didn't know anything about it. I can't say I'm happy about it. Makes me look like an idiot."

"Mark Nash is the idiot. Anyway, everything's good here. Have a great time. See ya."

"Dad's with Yummy?" This from Georgia.

"My, my," Paula says.

The twins leave in search of GUPPIE. JW paces around the house trying to decide what to do. He tries to phone Niki but Mrs. Sanjay reminds him that Niki works at Crummie's on Sunday. JW hangs up. Booger is his normal shape. He and Eric and Ringo are playing some game that involves a tennis ball and stairs. The phone rings.

"Hello, is Dr. Martin there? This is Jon Jennings from the *National Enquirer.*"

JW gives him Mark Nash's unlisted phone number.

The next three calls are the same but the fourth call is from Gloria.

"Hi, JW. I wondered if you'd like to come over?"

JW stares out the kitchen window. ZZ Top, the baby komodo dragon, is lumbering across the backyard chasing a butterfly. JW tries to picture two-hundred-pound ZZ Top leaping into the air. It isn't going to happen. Gloria is still talking.

"My mom just made chocolate chip cookies."

If you're a boy, it's never a good idea to be thinking about two girls at the same time. It's like having one foot in the boat and the other on the dock. As the boat starts to leave you better go one way or the other or be a good swimmer. In fairness, JW wouldn't have been thinking about Gloria at all if she hadn't phoned and he certainly wouldn't be riding over to her house if she hadn't mentioned her mother's Chocolate Chip Cookies, probably the best on the planet. But he's bored and this way he can kill three birds with one stone.

He can waste time at Gloria's eating cookies, then ride to *The Pet Vet* and feed the inmates and after that ride down to Crummie's and have a milkshake with Niki. It's a good plan except JW doesn't know about the *fourth* bird in the bush.

The bird in this case is Douglas "Don't Call Me Dougie" Brown and the bush is the big azalea that sits at the corner of Gloria's verandah.

Dougie is waiting in the bush for JW to show-up so he can finally check out this new magic bicycle he's heard so much about. He would have already checked it out if it hadn't been for that dumb blue-butted baboon hiding in JW's closet.

Dougie's still convinced this bike has to be JW's Inventors' project and he wants to know all about it so he can carry out Ernie's ingenious plan. Especially as how Dougie's idea to invent the Douglas Brown No-Water Toilet has so far produced not the sweet smell of success but rather large amounts of the opposite.

Gloria knows Dougie's in the bush. She can see his battered orange bike helmet if she looks hard enough. Gloria's a willing partner in Dougie's plan because JW has made the fatal mistake of not *begging* for forgiveness.

Sure, he said he was *sorry* but he could hardly expect Gloria to forgive him so *easily*. And then, before she had time to *reconsider*, there he was *hugging* that Niki person in the gymnasium. Now Gloria was stuck with Dougie the Dipstick, and how fair was that?

JW wheels into Gloria's driveway. JW lies Bicycle Booger down on the grass, takes the verandah stairs two at a time and knocks on Gloria's door.

"Hi, JW. C'mon in."

JW looks back at Booger. Better not.

"Would it be okay if we ate the cookies out here? It's so nice out."

Practically every day in California is nice out, so Gloria takes this as JW's way of saying he doesn't want to be inside with her. Fine.

"Sure. Why don't we go out back?"

"Okay. Can I bring my bike?"

"STAY HERE. I'LL GET THE COOKIES."

This is in capital letters because Gloria says it LOUDLY so the Nerd in the Bush will know what's going on. A minute later she's back with a plate of cookies and two glasses of real lemonade. She sits down on the top step and JW sits beside her.

"Why aren't you at your mom's?" Gloria asks.

"We came home early."

"Must be cool hanging around Mark Nash."

"Sometimes."

JW tells her about going to *Uppity's*, about getting dressed-up.

"Paula and Georgia must have loved that," Gloria says picturing it.

JW continues.

"They had these high heels that must have been *this high* and I'm sure they've never worn high heels before and there they were walking around like they were born with the things."

Gloria laughs. "Boys know how to throw balls and how to punch people."

"Are you telling me cavewomen wore high heels?"

"Just on weekends."

It's kind of ironic that Gloria and JW should be talking about Neanderthals at this particular moment because it's this particular moment that Dougie chooses to come hurtling out of the azalea bush, beating his chest and yelling a war cry that is even less successful than the Douglas Brown No-Water Toilet.

He runs straight to JW's bike, picks it up and heads down the driveway throwing himself up into the seat as he goes.

Unfortunately for *Dougie*, the only being he manages to startle with all this kerfuffle is Booger. Booger, not sure what's going on, locks the front wheel and expands the back wheel big enough to flip Dougie into space.

Dougie has been *rejected* dozens of times but this is the first time he's been *ejected.*

He lands on his head in the driveway and lies still. Booger stands beside him a normal bike again and the fact that he doesn't have a kickstand probably won't be noticed.

The whole thing happens so quickly neither Gloria nor JW are quite sure what they just saw. Gloria speaks first.

"Do you think he's hurt?"

"He's twitching."

"What happened?"

"Are there any more cookies?"

❧

Niki is glad to see him. Today she's wearing black shorts with the sleeveless black t-shirt that has *Crummie's* in silver italic letters across the front with a pointed line underneath.

At Crummie's there's a different color outfit for each day of the week. Sunday is black. Monday is deep purple. Tuesday is tan. Wednesday is white. Thursday is yellow. Friday is fire engine red and Saturday is silver. Holidays are orange and lime-green. Crummie's sells a ton of t-shirts to visiting kids looking for a souvenir.

JW orders three fries and three moonshines.

It's beautiful at Crummie's. When the tide's out the beach stretches for fifty yards before it dips under the blue Pacific water. When the tide's in the beach is half as wide but just as beautiful. The beach itself is about a mile long and shaped like a croissant. At either end the Shipstead hills come right into the water so that when the tide is in you can't leave the bay without wading out.

There are houses at either end, most of them the original fishermen's cottages, now renovated and worth a fortune. Crummie's, formerly Hal's Fish Warehouse, is the biggest building on the bay. It's made of wood, with a silver metal roof, lots of windows, and big sliding wooden doors that open onto the beach. Around Crummie's is all the land Jack Granite owns or has options on.

All this is reason enough for JW to be unhappy about seeing Jack Granite's black Mercedes standing by itself in the parking lot. He doesn't want it mingling with the common cars, thinks JW. It occurs to JW, who likes to think about things, that Jack Granite probably lives his whole life like that, away from others. But he doesn't really know if that's true, he just doesn't want Jack Granite taking down Crummie's.

"Break time." Niki appears with JW's order and sits down beside him.

"Aretheseforme?" she says through a mouthful of French fry. JW smiles. "AndIbettheseareforBooger."

JW answers her by dropping a few fries down the open end of the pipe that holds the handlebars. Niki takes the lid off one of the moonshines and pours some down the hole. She bends over and whispers, "Hi Booger."

JW's pretty sure he hears a burp.

15

The Grove Street Emergency

JW doesn't know how he knows but he knows the two police cars that passed him on Harper, lights flashing, sirens wailing are going to 17 Grove St. By the time JW rides into the driveway there are four police cruisers and two fire trucks out front and a crowd of neighbors. JW's dad is talking to Sheriff Riley. His dad looks angry. Really angry. This is not a look JW sees often.

"JW, all the animals are gone."

JW isn't going to believe this till he sees for himself. Mick's cage is open. No Mick, no Stevie Nicks. Upstairs is empty. JW looks up Manfred Mann's tree but all he sees is darkening sky. He runs inside the house. Gerry is definitely not in his cage.

No Eric Burdon, no Ringo. The rest might wander off but not Ringo. He'd have to be kidnapped or... JW isn't going there. Even ZZ Top isn't in the backyard. But there's a hole cut in the chain link fence. ZZ wouldn't be far away.

Oh boy.

Booger!

JW runs back to the driveway. Bicycle Booger is still there.

Good boy, Booger.

Thank you, Mommy.

One of the patrolmen is talking on the radio.

"Hey Sheriff! Dwayne says the back door at *The Pet Vet* has been pried open. There's no animals there either."

123

℘

There's another element of his father's character that JW doesn't see often but when he does he's always impressed. His dad can *take charge*. He sees it mostly when his dad is called in by the police or firefighters to rescue some animal that has gotten itself in trouble. JW saw it in SF when his dad was called by the police to come to Henry's Pet Store in the Galleria Mall. It was three days before Christmas.

A disgruntled employee had apparently opened all the snake cages after picking up his last paycheck. By the time Dr. Martin arrived all the snakes were accounted for but the largest of them, the ball or royal python.

"What's a ball python?" JW wanted to know. Mr. Henry, the owner, had the answer to that.

"A ball python is unique among snakes because it can make itself into a tight ball and actually roll itself where it wants to go." JW had a vision of a snake ball hurtling down Harper. That'd be something. "They usually grow to six feet but Pharaoh is just over eight feet long."

"Pharaoh?"

"That's what I called him. My employees called him Monty. There's no way the snake's in the store. We've looked everywhere. If it's out in the mall, heaven help us."

JW watched the hoards of shoppers streaming by the door.

Oh my.

JW's dad searched the store till he was convinced Mr. Henry was right, the python wasn't there. Then he studied the shoppers as well. Dr. Martin turned to Mr. Henry.

"You sell puppies, right?"

"Right," said Mr. Henry.

"Bloodhounds?"

Mr. Henry ran for the phone. Twenty minutes later, Jake the bloodhound was weaving through shoppers hot on the scent.

"I feel like Sherlock Holmes," Dr. Martin said holding onto Jake's leash. Jake kept pulling till he came to the escalator.

"No way," Mr. Henry said but Jake wasn't listening. The bloodhound rode the moving staircase down to the lower floor. Dr. Martin was beginning to like this snake.

Jake kept following his nose until all at once he stopped and looked up. So did Jake's owner. So did Dr. Martin and Mr. Henry. So did the two policemen. So did JW.

There in front of them sat Santa Clause with a little boy in his lap and wrapped around them and Santa's velvet chair was Pharaoh, the eight-foot-long ball python.

"Merry Christmas," whispered JW.

The people around Santa weren't sure what was up. Was the snake supposed to be there or what? The little boy wasn't the least bit scared but Santa looked ready to retire. Or expire. Take your pick.

Dr. Martin walked slowly towards Santa talking in a soft voice. Harry Potter, like Valdemort, is a parselmouth, a person who can talk to snakes. Dr. Martin isn't that but he knows how to relax animals. Knows how not to startle them, how to keep them calm. Slowly, he approached the snake until he was so close he could reach out and touch the python. The snake started forward traveling up Dr. Martin's arm, across his shoulders and down the other arm. Dr. Martin brought his hands together and the snake stopped.

Santa smiled up at Dr. Martin.

"I don't know about you but I just got my Christmas present. Thanks."

Dr. Martin tried to buy the python from Mr. Henry but he insisted on giving it to him.

"Please, it's the least I can do. What a disaster that might have been."

"What are you going to name him, dad?" asked Georgia later that night.

"Gerry and the Pacemakers," said Dr. Martin.

"Who?"

JW was there the first time they saw Mick. The police had called Dr. Martin, could he come to Novato right away? There's a gorilla in the garage. When they got there it was easy to see what the problem was. The gorilla's cage hadn't been cleaned for weeks. His owner was in hospital and everybody else was too scared to go in the cage. The resulting mess had caused sores on Mick's back and rump. He was one upset gorilla.

But JW's dad talked to him, calmed him down, went in the cage and gave him a shot of tranquilizer. They cleaned Mick up and took him to the San Francisco Zoo but the male gorilla there wanted nothing to do with this newcomer. Dr. Martin took Mick home.

JW watches his dad put his hand on Sheriff Riley's shoulder.

"Okay Jim," says Dr. Martin, "here's what we're going to do. First off, none of these animals is dangerous. The python and the gorilla are both big but they won't hurt anybody. So what we need is to get all these patrol cars out of here and back on the street spreading the word for people to phone the station if they see anything.

"Unless the animals have been abducted or killed and I don't see evidence of either of those things, I think their cages have been opened and they've been shooed out. If that's the case they won't have gone far and they're just as liable to come back here as venture too far."

Sheriff Riley is about to say something but Dr. Martin shakes his head.

"Move the cars, now."

Sheriff Riley does as he's told. No way he wants to be the target of Dr. Martin's anger. Dr. Martin walks out to the crowd that has gathered in front of the house. In a calm voice he tells his neighbors that someone has opened all the cages and that the animals are loose. He tells them about each animal and explains why they live in the house and why they aren't dangerous. He then asks each of them for their help in finding the animals before any of them are hurt.

"These animals are like little children," Dr. Martin explains. "At first, leaving home is a big adventure. Then it gets dark. They get confused and then they get scared. They want to come home but they don't know where it is. They *need* your help. JW and I *need* your help."

Everybody comes forward then and shakes Dr. Martin's hand. They leave determined to be the one to find Eric Burdon, the blue-butted baboon or Gerry, the eight-foot balled python. It's something.

JW watches as his dad opens his car door and snatches his phone off the seat. There is something else now and JW is afraid.

"Cynthia Martin, please." His dad looks out into the street, waiting. "Listen to me and don't say a word. Someone has broken into the house and the clinic and let all the animals out. You tell that Mark Nash if one of these animals is hurt I am coming there and nothing will stop me. Goodbye."

Dr. Martin hangs up and punches in new numbers. He's calling Mrs. Babiuk, his nurse at the clinic.

"Helen, George here. Listen, someone has broken into the clinic and taken all the animals or at least let them out of their cages. I need you to go there now and see what's going on.... I know you don't work weekends Helen, but... but... You know what Helen? You don't work any day of the week, you're fired!"

More numbers, this time Yummy's.

"Hey there, thanks for the nice day... Listen, someone has let all the animals out, both here at home and at the clinic. I need someone to go to the clinic and straighten that out while JW and I round up these guys... you'd better warn Amanda about Eddie... Okay, thanks." Dr. Martin looks at JW.

"Any ideas?"

"Lots." JW puts his hand out for the phone. He pushes redial. "Yummy? It's JW. Get Niki to help you at the clinic and could you announce over the PA what's happened and tell everybody there to keep their eyes open for strange animals... sure, a reward would be great... bye."

The twins arrive in a flurry wanting to know everything. The phone rings, it's JW's mom. Dr. Martin listens and then hangs up.

"Your mother's coming."

It's JW's turn to take charge. "Georgia, go upstairs and find Manfred Mann. Check the roof. He's got to be up there somewhere or close by. Paula, your job is the two birds. They can't be far away either. Dad, you get the cordless and stay with the phones. If you go out, call in and leave messages. I'm going after ZZ Top."

JW pushes his bike through the garage and out to the back. If his dad thinks this is odd he doesn't say anything.

"Boog, we need to find the other guys. Turn into a... hockey stick... close enough. Now we're going to find ZZ Top. Can you smell him?"

JW feels a tug on the hockey stick. Alright! Booger the Bloodhound.

JW climbs through the hole in the fence into the Smiths' yard Booger leading the way. It's dark out but there's enough light from the houses to see. ZZ went for a swim and then down the side of the Smiths' house, around the fence and into the Gormans' yard. There he found a pile of compost hidden at the back. He ate all the new garbage and promptly fell asleep. This running away from home is pretty strenuous work, you know.

JW stares at the sleeping komodo dragon. One down, twelve to go.

Mr. Gorman helps JW roll the two-hundred-pound ZZ into the wheelbarrow.

"He won't bite, right?"

"He's full."

"What, he's got a gauge or something?"

"Trust me."

JW's dad is on the cordless. He gives JW a thumb's up when he sees ZZ in the wheelbarrow. He puts his hand over the mouthpiece. "Eric's been spotted over at the public school. He's playing soccer."

"Maybe the cops should look after Eric?"

A look of understanding passes between JW and his dad. His dad grins. "Good idea."

The phone rings. It's Georgia.

"I've got Manfred Mann."

"Where are you?"

"Up the radio tower."

Dr. Martin swears under his breath. None of the kids are allowed up on the steep roof of the house and certainly not up the old rusty ham-radio antenna tower he's been meaning to take down ever since he bought the house. He goes out front and shines his Coleman up towards the antenna.

He finds Georgia about two-thirds up. She's holding on with one arm, her other is around Manfred Mann who has one arm around Georgia's neck and the other is holding a cell phone up to Georgia's ear. Manfred would wave something if he wasn't so tuckered out from all that climbing.

"Did you know Manfred Mann has his own iPhone?" Georgia asks. "He was listening to some weather news from Australia."

"You're joking?"

"Maybe it belongs to whoever did this?"

"There's an idea."

Dr. Martin hangs up then punches in the fire hall number. "It's Dr. Martin. We need the bucket truck back here, quick. Thanks."

He shines his light back on Georgia.

"You okay?" he yells.

"I can go up, but I can't go down!"

"That thing won't hold me or JW. Don't move, the firemen are coming."

"Well Manfred, you wanted some excitement."

"No Mann, that was you actually. You wanted a *rash* as I remember."

"This is better than a *rash*, this is a *rush*."

"We were quite fast I think. That man tried to dislodge us with that rake and we were fast enough to escape."

"It helped that he fell off his ladder."

"I suppose. You don't think we startled him by dropping our banana on his head?"

"I imagine we did... it sure is nice of Georgia to be holding on to us like this."

"She's rescuing us."

"You don't say."

Yummy phones from the clinic.

"Niki's here and her mom. Mrs. Babiuk showed up but she left when she saw us. Niki does a good imitation of a *Babiuk in Flight* if you ever want to relive the moment."

In the background Dr. Martin can hear Amanda calling for Eddie.

"So far we've found two kittens in a dumpster behind Crystal's, that's it."

That leaves four dogs, two cats, one kitten and Florida, missing in action. Yummy wants to know if she should phone the owners.

If they drive around yelling Porkchop, Porkchop might appear. Dr. Martin doesn't want to do this but he agrees. Better to save the animals than to save face.

Paula appears clutching Alice Cooper, the scarlet ibis. She found him eating goldfish in Mr. Tokishima's Japanese garden. Paula knew to look there because she'd left the upstairs door open one day and that's where blind Alice had gone.

That day Paula had made Mr. Tokishima promise not to tell her father. Mr. Tokishima took it as a good omen that a blind, beautiful bird would come to his garden, so he agreed. The next day Paula brought him a dozen goldfish. Her dad would buy this time.

JW has fixed the fence in the backyard and given ZZ a treat for being so good. Now he and Bicycle Booger are heading for the public school to rescue Eric from the cops or vice-versa.

Then the phone rings and it's one of the two calls Dr. Martin has been hoping for. Mrs. Gordon, on Grand, has a big ball on her back porch, the ball looks like one of those string balls she used to have as a child only way bigger.

"My dog is barking at it. Is that okay?"

"It's not great. Can you get the dog inside?"

"Not without going outside."

"The snake won't hurt you."

"Tell my feet that. They're not moving."

"What number are you?"

"122."

"Put dog food out."

"The dog just ate."

"It's for the snake."

"Oh."

Dr. Martin is at 122 in less than a minute. The dog is still barking. There's a story of a dog barking inside a large snake but this barking certainly isn't muffled. The front door opens and there stands the elderly Mrs. Gordon.

"The snake is eating the dog food."

"That's good." Dr. Martin is heading for the backdoor. "If I go out there what will your dog do?"

"Try to bite you."

"What kind of dog is it?"

"German shepherd."

"What would happen if we let him out the side gate?"

"He'd run away."

Dr. Martin has an urge to eat this dog himself.

"What's its name?"

"Jack the Ripper."

Dr. Martin looks out the back door window. Jack the Ripper is on the steps furious at this strange thing that has just eaten his food. Gerry, on the other hand, has had it with all this loud barking. He has his head up in the air preparing to strike. Dr. Martin tears open the door, grabs Gerry's tail and pulls back as hard as he can.

One second Gerry is bravely facing his foe and the next he's flying backwards heading right for poor Mrs. Gordon whose whole life has not prepared her for this moment.

Mrs. Gordon falls over dead.

Well, she's not *dead*, but she's fainted dead away as they say. Dr. Martin loads Gerry into the Cherokee then goes back inside to revive Mrs. Gordon.

Yummy phones in again. She's called the owners. They're all coming. She's sent Niki and her mom to check out the alley again for the last kitten. Dr. Martin heads home. The bucket truck arrives. Dr. Martin shines his light on Georgia. His friend, Frank Reynolds, is in charge.

"Frank, do me a favor, will you? Send up the youngest, best looking guy you got."

Frank laughs. "Johnson!"

Paula arrives at the same time as her mother in the Ferrari. They're both crying. Cynthia, because she feels so far removed from all this, and Paula, because she's found Janis Joplin. She holds the bird's body out to her dad and he takes it. Janis Joplin is dead. Her neck is broken. Paula hugs her mother and sobs.

"Where did you find her?"

But Paula can't speak. Dr. Martin watches as Johnson, the young fireman, gently lifts Georgia and Manfred Mann into the bucket. Georgia's got such a great smile, he thinks. Dr. Martin strokes Janis' feathers and sighs. Happiness and sadness, two streams that always run side by side.

16

The Truth About Eric

There's only one river running at Victor Harding Public School and it's a torrent called LAUGHTER. Now there are almost as many kinds of laughter as there are people but this time we're talking about the kind of laughter that happens to us all but not very often. We're talking about the kind of laughter that hurts.

Your sides hurt, your belly hurts, your back hurts, your voice hurts, your eyes water, you can't speak, you can point but only till you double over again. In the end, you beg it to stop but pray that it won't. That's the kind of laughter that's happening at Victor Harding Public School and you can guess why.

Eric Burdon is *entertaining*.

Before we get into this there's something you should know.

Eric Burdon is *not* a blue-butted baboon.

Well, that's not right either. He belongs to the baboon family but he's actually a MANDRILL.

Say what, right?

Do you remember back at the beginning when Eric was messing around wearing all of JW's underwear? If you had read Eric Burdon, the blue-butted *mandrill* the whole story would have stopped dead.

Mandrill? What the heck is a mandrill? Dad, what's a mandrill?

That thing for making holes. I got one in the garage.

Mom! What's a mandrill?

They're singers, country and western singers.

See? But, what you got to know is, being a mandrill is way cooler than being a baboon. It's like the difference between a sports car and a family sedan.

Here's why.

A mandrill has this incredible bright blue and red muzzle that sticks out of its furry face and looks like it's been carved out of plasticine. And its butt is so red and so blue and so shiny you think the mandrill must sit in a bucket of nail polish every morning.

We're going to continue to call Eric a blue-butted baboon, but really he's a mandrill, and we're all better off for having cleared this up.

To start with Eric Burdon, the blue-butted baboon, did not end up at Victor Harding Public School by mistake. He heard people and he saw lights. The big game lights were on because a girls' soccer game was being played between the Shipstead *Shooting Stars* and the Bodega *Bandits*.

The *Bandits* were ahead one to nothing when Eric Burdon scampered on to the field and stole the ball. No one knew what to do at first but the last thing the *Bandits* wanted was to have the game not count on account of monkey business.

"Is that *your* mascot?" asked one of the *Bandits*.

"I thought it was *your* coach," shot back the *Shooting Star*.

The girls tried to surround Eric but he took this as a form of California line dancing and started into his funny dance, hand on hip holding the ball, other hand up in air, butt wiggling, head thrown back and forth, like a cleaning lady who's just won the $10 million lottery.

If this story had a soundtrack the song playing would be *Nothin' Shakin'* sung by the Beatles:

My pappie told me
There'd be times like these
There's nothin' shakin'
But the leaves on the trees

Eric's dancing got the spectators laughing and the cell phones wagging. One of the calls was to the police station.

By the time JW and Booger arrive on the scene the soccer game is over, *Bandits* 3, *Shooting Stars* 2. The Shipstead coach took care of Eric without much trouble. She suggested the girls play with two balls at the same time so that every time Eric grabbed one ball the play could continue with the other. When the game ended none of the players and none of the spectators wanted to leave for the simple reason that Sheriff Riley with three policemen and two policewomen had arrived to take care of the matter.

Early the next morning Sheriff Riley would say to his wife, "Trying to catch that darn baboon had to be just about the funniest thing I've ever seen. Everytime you'd dive at it, it'd jump in the air, land on your head. If we make it onto America's Funniest Home Videos we're shoe-ins. Gladys, you know anything about getting grass stain out of uniforms?"

Even JW, who has no intention of being happy because he's so worried about Mick and Ringo and Stevie and the animals at *The Pet Vet*, can't stop himself and bursts out laughing like everybody else. And Booger must think it's hilarious too because all at once the hard pipes in Bicycle Booger change to soft garden hose sending JW sprawling to the ground from where he stares up at the sky and laughs till he can't laugh anymore.

Then the sky goes dark and JW is looking up at a shiny blue butt. Eric is tired and ready to go home. JW hops on Booger, Eric climbs onto the handlebars and with waves to everybody including Sheriff Riley, they head home.

When JW gets back to 17 Grove St. his dad is in the driveway talking to his mother who's been crying. Nobody looks happy.

"Hey, JW. Eric okay?"

JW tells his mom and dad about the soccer field, then asks his dad about the other animals.

"Everybody's here but Mick, Ringo and Stevie. I figure they're together. P & G just came back with the raccoons. They were having a party in Mrs. Finney's garbage can."

Dr. Martin watches as an official looking car pulls into the driveway. Parking on the street behind it is the *On-the-Move Van* from City TV.

Dr. Martin turns back to JW. JW can see the anger rekindle in his father's eyes.

"Janis Joplin is dead. Broken neck. They must have thrown her out the window. Paula found her in the window-well."

JW looks at his mom then turns away. He can feel the tears coming but it isn't her fault.

"Still six missing at the clinic including Eddie. Yummy's got the owners driving around town."

Out of the official looking car steps Fred Langton from the San Francisco Society for the Prevention of Cruelty to Animals. He and Dr. Martin have worked together dozens of times. It was Fred who brought Janis Joplin to *The Pet Vet*. He nods at Cynthia and JW and sticks his hand out for Dr. Martin to shake. A young woman gets out of the car and joins them.

"George, this is Shari Winkler of the San Francisco Department of Human Services, Children's Division."

Ms Winkler is dressed up for a night on the town. This isn't it. But before she can say anything Linda White, the pretty reporter from City TV walks up the driveway with a cameraman behind her.

"Dr. Martin?"

JW watches as his dad breaks away from the others and walks down the driveway.

"You're on private property."

"I'd just like to ask you a few questions about the animals."

Dr. Martin studies the reporter bringing his anger under control.

"JW."

JW appears pushing his bike, Eric Burdon still straddling the handlebars.

"Tell these good folks about Eric at the public school. Maybe he could do his funny dance if he's not too tired."

Dr. Martin walks back to the three people waiting for him in the light of the garage. Now Cynthia is the one looking scared.

"So, Ms. Winkler, what can I do for you?"

"We've had a complaint at Human Services that with all the strange pets you keep around here your children and the neighborhood children aren't safe."

Dr. Martin snorts. "Georgia! Paula!" The girls come crashing downstairs covered in raccoons. "Put the Dave Clark Five back and bring Gerry here. He's in the back of the Cherokee."

The girls' eyes go wide. Their dad is always *so nice* but now he is so *angry* and they know it.

"So Fred, I suppose you're just along for the ride?"

The man beside Ms. Winkler smiles. He's never seen Dr. Martin so upset.

"Something like that."

Fred Langton and Dr. Martin study each other. They're like two gunfighters facing each other, their hands at their sides. Are you here to help me or attack me? That's what JW's dad wants to know. Fred Langton doesn't waver. We're friends, his eyes say. That's all you need to know.

Dr. Martin directs his anger back at the young woman from the Children's Division.

"And you, Ms. Winkler, I don't suppose you'll tell me who called you?" Ms Winkler looks decidedly uncomfortable.

"You know I can't."

Dr. Martin turns his stare on Cynthia. "I bet it wasn't a long distance call."

Ms. Winkler works out of San Francisco. Dr. Martin looks over at the City TV van. Eric is on the big screen doing his funny dance and it is funny judging by Linda White's laughter. Dr. Martin turns back and beckons to the twins standing behind Ms. Winkler to come closer. They're holding Gerry on their shoulders. Gerry is yawning. Big day, y'know.

Ms. Winkler turns to see who it is Dr. Martin is waving at. Gerry's large open mouth isn't twelve inches away.

Fred Langton catches her.

"Take her home will you Fred? Thanks."

Dr. Martin tells the twins they're staying home to run Command Central. JW can tell his dad wants his mom to either stay with the girls or go home. Dr. Martin gets in the Cherokee. Cynthia climbs in beside him. JW gets in the back with his hockey stick.

"What's that for?"

"Hitting whoever did this."

When they arrive at the clinic there are seven cars and the Crummie Burger pick-up truck in the parking lot. Yummy has her tailgate down and is feeding everybody pizza. Dr. Martin takes a piece.

"Pizza?" he says smiling at Yummy.

"When you serve hamburgers all day, pizza is a treat."

Yummy hugs Cynthia. They haven't seen much of each other lately.

"Thanks for this," says JW's dad. "How's it going?"

"Three more in. Florida is still missing and one kitten. All the owners are okay except the Haycocks. They just got in from New Zealand. They didn't like me waking them up."

"How about Eddie?"

Yummy shakes her head. "Everybody back at the house?"

"Still no Mick, Stevie or Ringo."

Yummy makes a face. Mick wandering around isn't good.

JW carries a box of pizza into *The Pet Vet*. He leans Booger, the hockey stick, up against the wall and puts a piece of pizza on the floor beside him. Niki is in the back room showing her mom the kittens. Amanda is holding Niki's hand. Niki gives JW a one-armed hug, introduces him to her mom. Amanda lets go of Niki's hand and heads out front towards her mother.

"How are things at home?" Niki asks.

"Three missing." JW doesn't mention Janis. Time enough for that later.

"Same here."

"Where did you find the other kittens?"

"In the dumpster behind Crystal's."

"Let's look there again. You'd think they'd be together."

JW grabs his dad's big flashlight and the three of them walk down the dark alley. The back door at Crystal's is open and a woman with wild hair is standing in the doorway smoking. Above her a sign says *Crystal's Clairvoyance, Fortunes Told, Palm Readings, Tea Leaves, Séances*. The woman with the wild hair looks at JW and laughs.

"You're right," she says. JW was thinking that being able to see into the future and smoking didn't go together. Like applying for the job of Fortuneteller on the *Titanic*.

"A kitten," she says. Then she points her cigarette above her head. JW looks up. Light is pouring out of the apartment windows above Crystal's. Music too. JW heads up the wooden stairway that leads to the apartment. There is a landing with a door and a window. JW knocks on the door. It's opened by a little Asian girl holding a small white kitten.

"Will it be okay?" asks Niki as they head back.

"Leaving the kitten? You bet."

They no sooner arrive back than Mr. and Mrs. Haycock pull into the parking lot, car horn blaring, arms waving. Florida flew home! She's never been out of the house but she knew how to find home. Now that's a cockatoo!

Yummy looks around. She walks into the clinic, comes back out. "Where's Amanda?"

Now everyone is looking around.

"Amanda!" Dr. Martin shouts.

JW runs into the clinic. Amanda isn't the only thing missing! *Booger!*

People are moving now. JW can hear footsteps going in all directions.

"Over here!" It's Niki's voice coming from the darkness behind the clinic, the opposite direction from where the kittens were found. JW turns on the flashlight and runs that way.

He finds Niki behind *Doyle's Car Center. Doyle's* is full of old automobiles waiting their turn to be made new again. JW shines the light. Niki is lying down on the concrete half under a rusty blue Studebaker. Amanda is on her knees beside her. Niki squirms back out. She's dirty but smiling.

"Eddie's in the catch basin. I'm too big to get there."

"I'm not," Amanda says.

Amanda crawls under 'til all you can see is the bottom of her sneakers beyond the far tire. JW feels the others coming up behind him. Then Amanda's sneakers go into reverse and out she comes pulling Shipstead's Most Ugly Dog behind her.

Amanda sits up. She looks like a mechanic's rag, all dirty oil and crumples. Eddie doesn't care. He gives her a big lick. Every eye for fifty feet swells up with tears.

As Amanda stands she picks up the hockey stick and hands it to JW.

"It led me here," she says.

Dr. Martin drives home. Georgia is in the garage. She's made a box for Janis Joplin and lined it with a piece of purple velvet. Mick's cage is still empty. Cynthia gets out of the car.

"I know you all think Mark is responsible for this but I know he's not."

No one says anything.

"I hope you find Mick." And with that JW's mom is gone.

Dougie can't sleep. Every time he falls asleep he has this dream where he's standing on a little platform staring down at what looks like a hot tub full of nerds. They're waving to him, telling him to jump, the water's fine. And every time the platform gets higher and the hot tub smaller. In the last dream it looks like a cereal bowl full of drowning mice.

Dougie hears a car stop in front of his house. A spinning red light comes through his window flashing on his puce green wall. Dougie looks out. It's Sheriff Riley. In his hand Dougie can see an iPhone. The one his mom has been looking for.

JW glances over at the clock. Midnight. The twins have gone to bed. There've been no phone calls for an hour. JW is sitting in Mick's bamboo swing staring out at the ocean. There is a big ship out there with lights sailing south towards San Francisco. His dad is out in the blackness driving around because he has to be *doing something.*

Booger is across JW's lap but he must be tired because the two ends of the hockey stick have drooped down till they're resting on the floor. JW swings the swing around. He remembers Booger and Mick dancing and smiles. Then he jumps up and shakes Booger.

Booger better be awake now. He and JW are a rocket heading down Harper. JW is so excited that Bicycle Booger catches his mood and starts changing tire sizes as they go. They hit a red light at Lofton but JW doesn't even think about slowing down. No point. No brakes. Good thing there are hardly any cars on the road.

The same thing happens at Harris. The light turns red and JW keeps going. Too late he sees the onrushing headlights but Booger saves the day by somersaulting over the back of the red pick-up truck. They take the last corner at Front and come screeching into Crummie's parking lot. Yummy is just closing up.

"Hey JW, everybody back?"

"Still missing Mick, Stevie and Ringo. But I got an idea."

"Shoot."

"Could you put this CD on your loudspeaker? Mick loves track 9. Maybe if he hears it he'll come here."

"We're not supposed to make any loud noise after midnight, but to heck with that. Not every night you get to serenade a gorilla."

JW and Yummy stare at each other. They are both picturing some of the Missing Links that hang out at Crummie's.

"I take that back," Yummy says.

A Shot of Rhythm and Blues is playing for the eleventh time when Sheriff Riley pulls into Crummie's parking lot. JW tells him what they're doing. Sheriff Riley doesn't say anything about turning the volume down but Yummy does anyway. Sheriff Riley tells JW about talking to Douglas Brown about the cell phone.

"He says he was in your garage looking for your magic bike and the gorilla grabbed the cell phone. He says he doesn't know anything about letting the animals out and I believe him. And I don't think we have to do anything else because his mother is going to kill him."

Sheriff Riley leaves and the next car to pull into Crummie's parking lot is Dr. Martin's Cherokee. JW's dad heard the music eight blocks away.

Crummie's is closed now but Yummy keeps the lights on and the CD playing.

Get a shot of rhythm and blues,
With just a little rock n' roll on the side,
Just for good measure...

They sit out on the beach. JW builds a fire. There are a million stars and just as many waves. The moon is a big crescent and the path it paints across the ocean sparkles like a river of diamonds. Booger has made himself into a picnic table and isn't the least bit interested in getting close to the fire. Any fire.

"How nice is this?" asks JW's dad. Yummy and JW know he means it but there is a sadness in his voice only time will heal.

Yummy is digging her bare feet into the sand. "Jack Granite wants to buy it all. Build condos and a shopping complex."

"Never."

"That's what I keep telling him, but he keeps coming back."

"He should be trying to save something this beautiful not ruin it." JW's dad pokes the fire then stops in mid-poke.

"Is it my imagination or is that picnic table *moving*?"

Yummy looks where Dr. Martin is pointing. JW looks too, he doesn't want to.

"Yes, it's definitely moving," answers Yummy. "In fact, I would say it's *gliding*..."

The picnic table picks up speed.

"...or even *flying*."

"That's not possible."

"You're right," Yummy says.

"Then *why* is it doing that?"

"The tide's coming in."

Dr. Martin is too tired to do anything but laugh.

"What's the tide coming in got to do with anything?"

Yummy says in a big voice,

"There is a tide in the affairs of men
Which, taken at the flood, leads on to fortune."

JW knows that, Shakespeare, *Julius Caesar*. He'd studied it last year. JW likes adults who can quote things.

"But it isn't anywhere near the water," JW's dad says.

"It soon will be."

Yummy is right. The picnic table whizzes across the sand and into the shallow water sending up a rooster tail of silver spray.

"That's beautiful," say Yummy and Dr. Martin together.

Nope, thinks JW, that's Booger.

The picnic table has moved so far, so fast, it's now disappeared into the darkness. JW is thinking of getting up when suddenly the picnic table reappears and now that it isn't out of sight, it's a sight for sore eyes, because, sitting on the picnic table, flying over the sand towards JW, Dr. Martin and Yummy, are those three veteran travelers, Mick Jagger, Stevie Nicks and Ringo Star.

17

Goodbye Janis Joplin

The Martins have buried animals before. You can't work around living things and not experience death. It was the stopping of life, the finality of it, that made you work so hard to keep things alive.

Dr. Martin told his kids, "People and animals should die of too much time, nothing else."

Georgia lowers the box she'd made into the hole in the backyard and JW covers it over. That's what none of them like about this. Janis didn't die of too much time. She died because some stupid human being tossed a parrot that couldn't fly out of a window.

"We love you Janis Joplin," Georgia says.

"You old hag," JW whispers.

And with that the tears flow for a friend they hope is now flying high in a brand new sky.

JW has taken the bus to San Francisco before but never by himself. He isn't by himself this time if you count Booger the Backpack.

JW smiles thinking about the flying picnic table. The funny thing is his dad and Yummy were so excited to see Mick, Stevie and Ringo that it wasn't until they were pulling into the driveway at home that JW's dad remembered the picnic table.

"JW, was that picnic table really flying?"

"It sure looked like it."

"That's not possible."

"I don't think I'd mention it to anybody else."

"I think you're right."

JW strides across the lobby of the Nash Building. Jarrod at security looks surprised to see him.

"Hey, JW, how's it goin'?"

"Good. How 'bout you?"

"Good, good. Your mom went out about an hour ago, not lookin' too happy I might add. Mr. Nash is in L.A. Be back tonight."

"That's okay. I'll just be a minute. I was working on my science project all weekend and then I went and forgot it upstairs. Need it tomorrow."

"I used to forget science projects too. That's why I'm workin' here."

JW rides the private elevator up to the penthouse. He knows the number code to get in the front door. What he doesn't know is how to get into Mark Nash, Famous Rock Star and Rotten Person's private office. He has to at least try. He's sure it's Mark Nash that is causing all this trouble he just needs proof.

His dad is sure too. "That thing with the foundation. That was to get me away from home so that you kids would live with your mother. You can bet that was going to be part of the deal."

"That foundation sounded like a good idea."

"Good idea, wrong reason."

"And letting the animals go?"

"Nash trying to make me look bad."

"You looked good."

"We did alright."

The penthouse is deserted. JW stops in front of the office door and unloads Booger the Backpack. Inside is every tool that JW thinks he might need to break into Mark Nash's private office. And if all else fails he's brought his dad's mini-chainsaw.

"Okay Booger. We're trying to get inside this room. It's got a seven digit..."

The door opens. Booger is standing inside the office peaking around the office door. He is back to being a jellybean.

"Booger, how did you do that?"

But even if Booger could have answered JW isn't listening. He's too busy looking at the stuff on the walls. Mark Nash is everywhere. There isn't one photograph that doesn't have Mark Nash's smiling face. Even the platinum CDs have Mark Nash's face in the middle.

JW thinks of 17 Grove St. It's covered in photos too, a ton of Beatles' stuff because his dad collects it, but there are lots of family photos too, lots of animal shots. 17 Grove St. is fun, this is something else.

"Hey Booger, are you hungry? See if you can find us some food."

JW sits down at Mark Nash's desk. The only picture here is one of Mark and Cynthia in the Ferrari. JW puts it face down. He opens one of the drawers. It's packed with files neatly labeled. Most of it is business stuff. In the top left drawer is an address book. JW flips through till he finds a Sal. Sal Colucci, 24 Dante Ave.

Booger arrives with a bottle of pickles and two tall cans of beer. They are in a pocket he's made in his middle like a kangaroo.

"Booger, two-week-olds don't drink beer."

JW reaches into Booger's pocket and pulls the beer cans out. They're empty.

Booger burps.

Oh boy.

JW goes out to the kitchen. Booger follows. There are two more empty beer cans on the floor. Booger the Boozer. JW finds two submarine sandwiches left over from the weekend and gives one to Booger. He opens a jar of pickles and pours the pickles into Booger's pouch.

"If you turn green and bumpy, it's my fault."

Back in the office, in the bottom right drawer JW finds half of what he's looking for. There's a file there labeled Hair. JW opens the file and is rewarded with a wonderful photograph of a younger Mark Nash with no hair. Well, he has hair but none on top where you'd like it. This photo is followed by a dozen photos showing Mark Nash's scalp in different phases of hair transplant. The whole process is red and ugly.

So much for Mark Nash's famous long, wavy blonde hair, thinks JW. The trouble is JW isn't the kind to enjoy prying into someone else's life. This whole thing is making him feel red and ugly too.

But he's still determined to prove to his mother that Mark Nash has engineered the releasing of the animals and the calling of Human Services, Children's Division. JW puts his feet up on the desk and eats his sub. He can hear Booger in the exercise room doing something. It's probably better not to know.

JW sits up. There is one of those leather green blotter things on the desk that has obviously never been used. He picks up the edge knowing there isn't anything underneath it but while he's confirming this he might think of something else. But there is something there.

JW flips the desk pad over.

The underside is the same as the top except it's covered in doodles. Hundreds of them. Drawn by Mark Nash while he's talking on the phone. JW doesn't have to look hard to find what he wants. The whole middle of the green blotter is covered in animals. A snake, a gorilla, a parrot, even an attempt at a blue-butted baboon. And there in the midst of the animals is scrawled a name and a number. Shari Winkler, 937-8946. The woman from Human Services.

That's it. JW pulls the marked green blotter out of its corners and flips the desk pad over. He writes two words on the top, Nice Hair. He takes the *Hair* file and locks the office door behind him.

Booger is boxing, sort of. He's hitting one of those little punching bags that you smack with one hand and then the other as fast as you can. Booger is hitting it with the top of his body and every time he hits it it bounces back and punches Booger. This is happening so fast it's hard to see each blow but from what JW can see the punching bag is winning.

JW goes to his mom's bathroom and puts the green blotter in the top drawer.

"Booger, let's go!"

JW walks back to the exercise room. He's just in time to see Booger spin like a corkscrew and topple to the floor.

Dante Avenue is one of those little streets down by the Market. 24 is a duplex and Sal Colucci has the top floor. JW rings the bell. The door clicks open. He walks up the stairs. He isn't scared but he thinks he probably should be. The door at the top of the landing opens and a man shaped like a fireplug comes out wearing a suit and carrying a bottle of beer. JW feels Booger the Backpack shudder. Booger isn't feeling so good.

"And you would be?"

"John Martin, Dr. Martin's son."

"And I should know you?"

"You were in my house yesterday."

"Not me."

"You killed our parrot."

JW pushes past Sal into his apartment. JW isn't sure why but having Booger on his back is making him brave. Sal seems amused.

"Make yourself at home."

"I will."

JW looks around the living room. It's tidy which surprises him. The furniture is okay, nothing flashy. JW pulls Booger off his back and dumps all the tools onto the carpet.

"Building something?"

"I thought I might have to break into Mark Nash's office but the door was open."

"Nice of him."

JW picks up Booger and tells him he needs to be a hockey stick. Fireplug watches as the backpack transforms itself into the desired item. This would have been impressive except the hockey stick is green, and undulating in JW's hand like a captured snake. Booger is definitely drunk.

"Is that one of those transformer things? Man, what'll they think of next."

JW isn't listening. He's heading down the hallway letting Booger the Intoxicated lead the way. Booger hiccups in each doorway but he picks up speed when he enters the last bedroom. He heads right to the closet door and stops. JW reaches for the handle. He can feel Sal behind him.

"I wouldn't do that if I was you."

JW opens the door. There hanging on a hook is Mick's pink evolution t-shirt.

In his dreams JW punches Sal hard enough to knock his teeth out. In reality, he puts the tools and Mick's t-shirt in Booger the Backpack and starts towards the door.

"I'm sorry about the parrot, kid. I thought it could fly."

JW stops and stares at Sal.

"She flew once. That's more than you'll ever do."

With that JW runs down the stairs out into the sunshine.

18

Big Pink

Things will never be quite the same at 17 Grove St. but they are heading towards near normal at a speed that surprises the family that lives there.

People Without Brains are still phoning to report seeing a Giant Snake carrying off a Large White Poodle but it might have been an Alligator carrying an Albino Sheepdog with a Bad Haircut.

The odd reporter still calls to ask about the Mark Nash Foundation and what affect it will have on the extinct animals in Iowa.

JW's mom calls to say she's sorry for all that's happened. She's moving into a hotel while she straightens things out. As the three kids are never going back to Mark Nash, Famous Rock Star and Confirmed Rotten Person's penthouse, this is probably a good idea.

Dr. Martin sleeps in Thursday morning. The night before he took Yummy to see the new musical, *Drums*, in San Francisco and didn't get in till late. He is still only half awake as he stumbles into the kitchen. One look and he almost stumbles back to bed. He's forgotten today is Halloween and in Shipstead Halloween is the most serious of celebrations.

What almost sends him back to his warm covers is the sight of the twins dressed up as Martians. They might be *Dragonflies*

Without Wings or even *Salad Tongs* but Dr. Martin is pretty sure they're Martians. To add to the confusion they are being interviewed by JW, the CNN reporter, and a cameraperson wearing Dr. Martin's hot pink overalls from the garage. Probably Miguel or Ty thinks Dr. Martin.

"So, how do you like the air here on earth?" JW asks as his dad enters.

"We."

"Like."

"It."

"All."

"Right."

At this point the two Martians bow to each other and giggle like Japanese schoolgirls.

"A."

"Bit."

"Stale."

"Per."

"Haps."

"But."

"Once."

"Earth."

"Lings."

"Are."

"E."

"Lim."

"In."

"A."

"Ted."

"It."

"Will."

"Be."

"Hunkey."

"And."

"Dorey."

"Hi."

"Dad."

Hi Dad has to laugh despite the two woodpeckers fighting inside his head.

"You guys look great."

In fact, Dr. Martin is a little worried about *how great* his little girls look. They're wearing spandex body suits they'd bought with their mother last weekend. Georgia's is a bottle-green color and Paula's is cool silvery-blue.

The suits have hoods that cover the girls' heads like bathing caps and out of the ear holes the twins have managed blond pigtails and on top they have matching red hair bands with floppy antennae.

The girls put an arm around each other's waist and the other two they stick out like show girls.

"I'm O."

"I'm Kay."

"And together we're... O'Kay."

Even JW laughs at this. He is wearing baggy brown chinos, brown lace-up shoes, a blue shirt, bright red tie and a brown tweed sports jacket he's borrowed from his dad's closet along with a fedora hat. He looks like a young Indiana Jones. He pushes the hat up and turns to his dad.

"And I'm Clark Kent and this is my assistant, Big Pink."

JW knows his dad will like this because he listens all the time to The Band's *Music From Big Pink*. And Big Pink makes sense because Booger is not only wearing the hot pink overalls from the garage but Mick's pink evolution t-shirt and a pink baseball hat JW's borrowed from Paula.

The pretend TV camera JW has made from pieces of plywood which he's spray-painted pink. Inside is a real camera. He doesn't know how Booger is going to push the button but that's Booger's problem. To top it off Booger has made his skin look like thick pink latex with a pretty girl's face and oodles of long dark pink spaghetti hair.

There's one more thing you should know.

Booger is *shaped* like Barbie.

"So, Dr. Martin, I notice you're not looking your usual chipper self and that you are considerably later rising than is your norm. Perhaps you would like to account for your miserable appearance?"

JW holds out the microphone.

"I'm taking the fifth."

"I'd say you'd be better off taking two Tylenols."

"You're probably right. Who's Big Pink?"

"He."

"Won't."

"Tell."

"Us."

JW doesn't want to spend too much time on this.

"Got... to... go!"

JW loves Halloween at Shipstead High. Everybody takes part. Teachers, janitors, cafeteria staff, even those kids too cool to dress up think better of it. Being cool without an audience doesn't work at all.

This year Mr. Haywood, the principal, is Zorro. His secretary, Ms. Hernadez, is a beautiful senorita, in a bright red flamenco dress with enough crinolines for a prom.

JW is having a good time interviewing everybody he bumps into.

"So, Senor Zorro, you are surrounded by soldiers, your sword is broken, your whip is cut in half, your horse is lame, what do you do?"

"I yell, 'Has anyone seen Zorro?'"

"So, Tonto, who do you go to when you need money?"
"The Loan Ranger."

"So Batman, how do you feel about Robin?"
"It beats workin' for a living."

"So, Colonel Mustard, what's it like to be done in by Ms. Peacock in the library with the knife?"
"You mean I'm dead?"
"I believe so."
"I knew I was spread *too thin*."

"So, Sherlock, was there ever a question you couldn't answer?"
"Yes, Watson, there was."
"What was it?"
"How stupid can you be?"

Booger is having a great time. It's the first time he's been out as something living. Sure he has Dr. Martin's overalls on, Mick's evolution t-shirt, Paula's baseball hat and a shape like Barbie but still he's himself. The shape like Barbie is certainly arousing attention.

"JW, who's in there?"
"No way that's a guy. No way."
"Do I know you? I'd like to."
"My dreams have come true."
"Hi, I'm Ken."

They sit beside Niki in the cafeteria. She is Cleopatra and if there's a list for head slave JW is signing up.

"So, Cleopatra, how did you Mark Antony?"

"With Caesar Salad?"

JW hopes Booger's camera is still operating. He wants to give Niki a picture of Cleopatra for Christmas.

"You look fantastic!" JW says meaning it.

And Niki does. She has on thirty colored see-through scarves with a two-piece black bathing suit underneath and lots of gold jewelry around her neck and her arms, but the best piece is the gold snake coiled around her forehead, the snake's head up ready to strike.

"Nice asp," JW says grinning.

"Thanks, I think. Speaking of fantastic is that Boog?"

"Better known as Big Pink."

"She's too cute."

"She's having a *really good* time."

"I bet."

Just then Bob Pendergast, dressed as a Roman Centurion, sits down on the other side of Niki. JW has to admit Bob looks pretty good.

"Hey Niki, we should go to the party together. Y'know, Antony and Cleopatra."

"Sorry Tony, I'm being interviewed *all night.*"

JW carries that smile around *all afternoon.*

Everything is smooth until they hit biology class. Mr. Barber, JW's biology teacher, has come to school as an amoeba. He looks like a giant silver jellybean with silver arms and legs. He has a silver bathing cap on. Even his moustache is silver.

JW can tell Booger is having trouble making sense of this shoddy look-a-like. And if that isn't bad enough when JW asks Mr. Barber,

"So, Amoeba, may I call you that?"

Mr. Barber answers, "My friends call me Booger."

The class thinks this is very funny. Amid the laughter Booger's camera turns towards JW. JW can feel himself blush.

Oh, Booger, I'm so sorry.

"Ah, and what will we be learning today?" JW asks trying to change the subject. All day Booger has been content to stay beside JW but now he's moving around Mr. Barber checking him out like a dog at a fire hydrant.

"Today we will be learning how a simple single-celled organism reproduces itself by dividing."

JW wants to be anywhere but where he is.

JW walks to the back of the class and keeps going out the rear door. With half the class standing up because their costumes won't let them sit down JW is sure Mr. Barber won't notice his departure. He is ten steps down the hall before he realizes Booger isn't with him.

Back he goes. Booger is standing by the rear door, behind Ellie McPherson who is dressed up as a Big Red Tomato. She even has a puffy, spiked green hat. She turns and smiles at JW. He gives her a thumb's up.

At least Booger isn't at the front sniffing Mr. Barber.

"We've talked about the origins of life. How billions of years ago an atmosphere made up of hydrogen, water vapor, ammonia and methane was subjected to electrical discharges and ultraviolet light.

"How this combination produced organic compounds such as phosphates, enzymes and nucleic acids and how these compounds were later surrounded by membranes making them into the first cells."

JW looks over at Booger. Booger has his camera on and is capturing every word Mr. Barber is saying.

"But I don't want you to think of these single cells as *simple*. They're not. You're made of them and we know you're not *simple*.

"In fact, they are machines of *staggering complexity* and *stunning beauty*.

"Consider that a single cell carries all the genetic material necessary to create a unique human being. Consider that this human being that starts from a single cell ends up with ten million million cells each with their own job to do. Your body has twenty square feet of skin, 100,000 hairs, ten fingernails, two eyeballs, one tongue, two ears, a nose, a liver, a brain, *a heart*.

"All from a single cell."

Mr. Barber, like any good teacher, lets this sink in.

"All cells have some things in common. Each 'breathes' in its own way, takes in food, gets rid of waste, grows, reproduces itself and dies. Today we're only concerned with the reproduces itself part.

"In basic terms what happens is our single cell grows to twice its size and divides in two. These two cells grow and divide and so on. The wonderful part is that before each cell divides, it makes a second complete set of genetic material, its DNA, so that each cell when it divides will know what to do."

JW knows what's going to happen before it happens. Booger's thoughts are so strong they are flooding JW.

Booger is going to divide.

JW shuts his eyes like a little kid thinking that what he can't see can't happen.

But when he opens them it has happened. Beside Booger stands another silver jellybean. Not as big as Booger but close. JW has the feeling this new Booger is a girl. He doesn't know why he thinks this anymore than why he thinks of Booger as a boy.

"I know it's Halloween and that I don't have your *undivided* attention... but there is one thing I'd like you to think about between now and next class.

"Men and women have been studying and thinking about *life* since the beginning of time. Despite all this thought there is still no generally accepted definition of life."

JW watches as the second Booger disappears back into Booger. Ellie, the Big Red Tomato, turns and smiles at JW. He smiles back and wills her to turn back towards the blackboard.

Ah man, Booger, don't do it.

Too late. JW looks over and now there are at least a dozen little jellybeans moving around Booger. JW pulls on Booger's sleeve and whispers.

"Not now Booger. We'll do this at home."

Mr. Barber looks around at his students.

"If we go back to our amoeba, let me ask you this? What is it that drives our not so simple single cell to reproduce itself? There is no need to. There is no benefit to the original cell in making a copy of itself.

"But I can tell you that I have a son and a daughter and they are the most precious things in the world to me... so I ask you, isn't this drive to share ourselves the key to all things? Isn't this drive to reproduce the *essence* of life itself?"

This would have been a great line to end the class on except the effect is ruined by a loud scream from the Big Red Tomato at the back of the room.

But it's hard to blame Ellie because at the moment she's covered in silver slug-like beings, the size of zucchinis, one of which is sitting on her green spiked hat looking over the edge into her eyes.

Booger, don't do this!

JW listens to the sound of turning as everyone is curious to see what has made Ellie scream. The little Boogers are spreading out now, scurrying up the back wall and ceiling darting back and forth like things do when you look at slime mold through a microscope. No one says a word until finally JW yells out, "Way to go, Booger!"

JW starts clapping, whistling, pointing at Mr. Barber who is as amazed as his students by what he is seeing. "Fantastic! What's that?" JW points at the corner of the classroom to the left of Mr. Barber and everyone turns back to see what new wonder has appeared.

JW's loud voice seems to finally penetrate some part of Booger's being enough that he recalls all his offspring back into himself.

When everyone turns again JW and Big Pink have vanished!

19

Twick or Tweat!

Jack Granite is all set. In the trunk of his car he's stashed his gloves, his ski mask, a can of gasoline and a lighter. He doesn't have an alibi but he's decided involving someone else in this is way more risky than saying he spent the evening alone at Shipstead House. "If I was going to burn down Crummie's don't you think I would have gotten myself an alibi?"

Besides it's Halloween, it'll look like kids did it.

I'm sorry Yummy, but I've got to do something.

"Hey Paula, we need more stuff!" JW is at the back door of the garage yelling at the silvery-blue Martian in the kitchen window. Paula waves. As usual on Halloween 17 Grove St. is packed.

There must be thirty twick or tweaters — as Paula used to say when she was little — gathered at the bars of Mick's cage. Mick has his Scary Sounds CD going, we are now at *Skeleton Being Dragged Through Graveyard*, and Eric Burdon is inside with Mick wearing his black cape and Zorro mask striding around flapping his arms like a demented fruit bat. Mick hands out the treats.

Stevie looks at a three-foot Mickey Mouse and thinks, *Why would you be anything but a cat?*

"We get more every year," Dr. Martin says shaking his head as if next year he'll have to take out a loan to pay for all the treats. Yummy laughs.

"If you were a kid wouldn't you want to come here?"

"I guess."

"You should hand out business cards."

Dr. Martin puts his arm around Yummy.

"Then the business could pay for the treats. How would you like to be my accountant and my assistant?"

JW sees the hug and smiles. His dad hasn't had much luck with women since his mom left. This looks better.

Georgia comes downstairs carrying Manfred Mann and Amanda has one of the Dave Clark Five perched on her shoulder hanging on for dear life. They head for the driveway to share their animals with the other kids.

"I wish we could dress up," says Mann in the arms of a nine-year-old ballerina.

"That would be fun," says Manfred. "What would we be?"

"An elephant."

"Ach JW, if I'd been wantin' to make an impression I'd've come as a ballpeen hammer."

Ty is talking into JW's microphone. It's quarter to nine. They're at Shipstead High in the hallway outside the gymnasium waiting for the dance to begin. Ty is wearing black jeans, a black turtleneck and black boots. He has a silver hoop earring and a nose stud and enough gel in his hair to lubricate a backhoe. On his head is a tinfoil crown. Sticking out the back of his jeans are a hundred shiny silver nails. He looks like a punk porcupine.

"Perhaps you'd like to share with our audience the significance of the rather large pincushion you're wearing?"

"It's symbolism. True artists dunna show you what they see they show you what they feel about what they see. Can you no see that?"

Like most of the boys at Shipstead High, Ty is having trouble taking his eyes off Big Pink.

"JW, I canna stand it no longer. Is Big Pink someone I know? Because you got me heart pounding here and I'm hoping there's a girl in there somewhere that I can be practicin' me charm on."

JW is grinning and Booger's camera is shaking.

"All things are possible to those who dream," JW says. "Now please tell everybody out in TV land just exactly who you are."

"I would a thought it was a no-brainer. I've come as myself, A Royal Pain-in-the-Butt."

JW thinks the gymnasium is *amazing*. When you walk in you feel like you've landed in Yoda's swamp just like Luke Skywalker did so many movies ago. There is creepy stuff hanging everywhere and somewhere a mountain of dry ice is making clouds of spooky mist.

Luke Skywalker's X-Wing fighter is sticking out of the swamp and its colored flashing lights make a strobe effect in the fog that has you looking around for Darth Vader or worse. The final touch is a soundtrack of something big, walking in something wet, dragging something you definitely don't want to meet.

Oh man Booger, this is so good!

It takes JW a few minutes to find Cleopatra. She's surrounded by boys which doesn't surprise him. JW pushes his way through and sticks out his microphone.

"Cleo, about that interview."

"Yes, Darling, I've been waiting for you. Big Pink, I heard you were a naughty girl in biology class."

Booger's camera nods up and down enthusiastically.

At nine o'clock the music starts. Dracula, the disk jockey, gets things rolling with *Bad Romance*. JW dances every dance with Niki. One by one his friends check in. Miguel is the Wicked Witch of the West from the Wizard of Oz.

"I told my dad I was going as my stepmother — just kiddin'. Have you seen the Royal Pain?"

During *Only the Young* JW sees Gloria (Amelia Earhart wearing a leather flying jacket and jodhpurs) stomp by dragging Dougie wearing his astronaut's suit. She looks wistfully at JW but he has his arm around the only partner he wants. Beside Cleopatra everyone else is Second Prize.

Boys keep asking Big Pink to dance. As usual Booger learns quickly and is soon the best dancer in the gym.

"How does he do that?" JW asks. "He's so good at everything."

"Maybe he's a girl," answers Cleopatra grinning.

The last dance is a slow one, *For Now, Forever.* JW and Niki want just that. At the end JW looks over at Booger. He's dancing with the other Booger from biology class. As the last note fades away the two Boogers melt together.

But Halloween in Shipstead isn't finished yet. There is at least one more trick to go. The dance is over and kids are heading home. But JW and Niki aren't ready to go their separate ways. Niki phones her mom and gets permission for JW to walk her home. JW phones his dad and gets the usual "one hour."

But they don't walk home. Instead they head towards the beach at Crummie's. For one thing it's downhill, for another they have enough money to call a cab to take them home and thirdly, they want to be someplace beautiful to end this beautiful night.

Ahhhhhhh.

Crummie's is closed when JW and Niki get there. The lights are off. The only noise is the waves rushing towards the shore. There is a big log lying halfway between Crummie's and the ocean and JW and Niki settle there, their backs against the warm wood.

Booger is hanging back like the third wheel on a bicycle. He still has his pink clothes on but he's not shaped like Barbie anymore. He's back to being himself. JW gets up and gives Booger a hug.

"C'mon Boog, there's room for all of us."

JW leads Booger to the log and Niki pats the sand. Booger folds up beside her. Niki puts her arm around his back and pulls him close. She does the same to JW.

"I love you, JW. I love you, Booger."

We don't know how many millions of stars there are in the sky but this night they are all trying to be the brightest, the best. Two shooting stars appear at the same time, their paths crossing like a giant X. Niki leans her head on JW's shoulder.

"My dad's a soldier," Niki says. "I've lived in eight different places so far. I used to think every time I made a friend that was the signal to move."

JW thinks back to Janis Joplin saying your mother wears army boots. No wonder that hurt.

JW can tell there's more but this is a first step for his new best friend of the human variety. JW kisses Niki's hair and the moment passes.

It's almost time to go when Booger starts sniffing. Then JW smells it too. Gasoline. JW stares over at Crummie's. For an instant he sees a shadow move at the corner of the building. Then there's a spark and Crummie's bursts into flames.

"Hey!"

JW is up and running before the others realize what is happening. I shouldn't have yelled thinks JW because now the shadow is running too into the darkness, away from him, and at considerable speed. It's somebody dressed all in black. He turns once to see if JW is gaining. It's a man wearing a black ski mask. He disappears into the shadows. No way JW's going to catch him. Doesn't matter anyway it's the fire that counts.

Booger flies by on JW's right. The pink clothes are gone and as JW sprints towards the fire Booger changes from a jellybean to a giant Manta Ray. His wings are so huge when he passes JW, JW can no longer see the flames.

"No Booger, no!"

JW's cry does no good. The giant Manta Ray lands on the corner of Crummie's its wings totally extended. JW can see Booger shudder with pain as his wings smother the flames. Then Booger is gone again a silver bullet rocketing into the darkness.

"Did you see that?" Niki is beside JW. JW has his jacket off. Every time a flame reappears he smothers it with his jacket. His dad's jacket.

"We need water."

"Not with gasoline. Try throwing sand."

In the distance they hear a car start and the squeal of tires.

"Booger was amazing!"

"I can't believe he did this," JW says. "Not after his last fire."

"Did you see who it was?"

"No. I shouldn't have yelled."

Niki bends down and picks up a cheap plastic lighter. She holds it up for JW to see. It doesn't take Niki long to find the empty gas can. Booger reappears wearing the black ski mask. He's shaking badly and has that burnt coffee smell again.

"You okay, Boog?"

Niki gives Booger a hug. "You saved Crummie's, Booger. What you did was incredible." Niki and JW look at each other. Crummie's was made of wood and over a hundred years old. It wouldn't have lasted twenty minutes.

"Guy got away?"

Booger makes an arm and holds out his hand. Booger's made it big and flat, the size of a car license plate. Imprinted in his hand is the word GRANITE.

20

The Vanishing Villains

Gerry heads up the stairs. It's early morning and most mornings Dr. Martin lets him out to get some exercise. Gerry thinks he'll visit JW see if the new guy wants to dance again. *Oops. There's Georgia. Better stop, don't want to startle her.* Gerry pushes on JW's door and slithers in. Gerry raises his head to the level of JW's bed.

"Hey Gerry. How's it goin'?"

JW rolls out of bed, shuts his bedroom door, crawls back into bed. There's no point in getting up till the bathroom is free. The bedroom door opens and closes. Eric Burdon waltzes in. This is starting to look like a party.

"Hey Boog, wake up. Gerry and Eric are here."

JW stares up at the ceiling. He has a lot to think about. Inventors is next weekend and JW is worried about Booger. Winning Inventors without betraying Booger is going to be tricky.

Jack Granite hasn't been dealt with.

JW doesn't know what's going on with Mark Nash and his mom. Or his dad and Yummy for that matter.

But he knows how he feels about Niki and it's like winning the basketball game. Except now that they are best friends he can worry that someday they won't be. Have you noticed there's never a shortage of things to worry about?

Booger and Gerry are doing their skipping rope dance with Eric

Burdon caught in the middle. He looks like a stuffed toy going round and round in a dryer. JW can see dark patches on Booger's skin but once again Booger seems to be healing quickly.

Winning Inventors without Booger is next to impossible thinks JW. There isn't enough time to put together something brilliant. But winning with Booger could be a disaster. If people figure out what they're looking at Booger's life will never be the same. Every scientist on the planet will want to test him, prod him, measure him, extract him, even cut into him.

But who is JW to deny planet Earth its first Alien Being?

But Booger is his buddy.

But what if testing Booger could lead to a cure for cancer or something?

But Booger trusts him.

But JW would win Inventors. He'd whoop Dougie Brown's butt once and for all.

But Booger is his *friend* and that's more important than winning.

JW's thoughts circle back to Jack Granite. JW stopped Niki phoning the police last night. Then she wanted to call Yummy and JW stopped that too.

"We need to think about this," he told her. "Granite won't come back now. And we can't really prove anything. I mean we can't say my Alien Being captured Granite's license plate on his hand except he doesn't really have hands."

Niki agreed, reluctantly.

"We'll tell Yummy tomorrow."

But now it's tomorrow and JW still isn't sure what to do. If they tell Yummy she'll go to the police and JW and Niki will have to lie to protect Booger. JW goes to the kitchen and comes back with the cordless phone and the phone book. Eric Burdon has escaped from the dryer. Now he's staggering around dizzy from his ride. Booger and Gerry are still at it. JW dials.

"Mr. Granite? My name is John Martin. I'm the one who saw you last night at Crummie's with the gasoline. There are two other witnesses and we have your ski mask, your lighter and your gas can."

There is a lengthy silence and then the strong smooth voice that JW knows from TV.

"I gather you haven't gone to the police?"

"Not yet. I thought I might accomplish what I want without them."

"And what is it you wish to accomplish?"

JW has the feeling Mr. Granite is amused by the word accomplish.

"Two things. First, I want you to forget about Crummie's. That whole waterfront is beautiful just the way it is. Any development there would be a huge step backwards."

More silence. JW can feel Jack Granite looking down from his mansion on the hill.

"Okay. What's number two?"

"I'm not sure yet."

"Is it money?"

"No."

"Good."

JW calls Mark Nash.

"JW, thanks for calling. I guess I screwed up big time. Sorry."

"I've got your hair file."

"To be honest JW, that's old news."

"We're not coming there any more."

"Your mom's moved out. I'm trying to talk her into forgiving me. You could help."

"Why would I?"

"Because we all make mistakes, because only the strong forgive... to err is human, to forgive, divine."

JW is quiet thinking about this. He wants to hurt Mark Nash for killing Janis Joplin and for trying to cause trouble for his father.

Mark Nash comes back on.

"By the way, JW, what did you do to my friend Sal?"

"What's that?"

"Sal said you came over, said you two talked. I don't know what you said but Sal doesn't want to work for me anymore."

JW doesn't know what to say to this.

"He also said you left behind the biggest pile of crap he's ever seen."

Booger strikes again.

Have you noticed how hard it is these days to find a good villain? There are only so many Voldemorts to go around. Here we were with *four* villains, two of them with real potential and what have we got?

Mark Nash is sorry and wants JW's help.

Jack Granite agrees to leave Crummie's alone.

Sal is going to teacher's college so he can be the guidance counselor at Shipstead High.

Maybe not but you get the idea. So that only leaves us with Douglas "Don't Call Me Dougie" Brown and he wasn't much to start with.

It's a good thing another villain, a real villain this time, is about to step up to the plate *and* to make things even more interesting the FBI is about to discover Shipstead, California.

Sheriff Riley holds the phone away from his ear and looks at it. It looks like it always did. That is reassuring.

"I don't understand why you didn't phone us when these occurrences began," says Special Agent Angela Burns of The Federal Bureau of Investigation. "That's what we're here for."

It seems to Sheriff Riley that if Special Agent Angela Burns speaks any louder he'd hear her from San Francisco without the telephone.

"Which occurrences would these be?"

"Sheriff Riley, have you been listening to me?"

"I didn't know I had a choice."

Silence. Sheriff Riley looks at his calendar. Three more years and he can RETIRE.

"There's the report of the strange bicycle. Then there's the rather large... deposit in Dead Man's Lookout. There's the flying picnic table. Then we have thirty little alien beings in a science class..."

"Could you hang on a minute, I've got another call coming in."

School is quiet like it always is after Halloween. After anticipation comes an equal but opposite reaction.

Booger the Backpack is subdued but he's caught the mood from JW. JW and Booger are now quite capable of walking around in each other's thoughts. Booger knows his mommy is worried about him he just doesn't understand why.

After school 17 Grove St. is quiet too. JW's dad is so preoccupied it takes JW three sentences before he realizes his dad hasn't heard a word he's said.

"Sorry, JW, my mind is a thousand miles away. What were you saying?"

"I was suggesting we have a picnic at Draper's Point."

JW and his dad stare at each other. Having a picnic at Draper's Point is code language for *I have something serious to tell you and I need to be someplace quiet with no interruptions.*

"Good idea. You tell the girls, I'll pack the picnic."

"Booger? You see dad's Jeep Cherokee? Can you turn yourself into that?"

He can. He does. He sort of.
JW parks his dad's real car in the last bay of the garage and closes the door. The red Booger-Cherokee is waiting in the driveway when Dr. Martin and the girls arrive. It's all JW can do not to burst out laughing.

The Booger-Cherokee looks okay if you don't look too hard. For instance, the side mirrors aren't flat but rippled. Booger is obviously having trouble duplicating things that pick up colors from the things around them. Like sky in the mirror.

When Paula pulls her door shut it doesn't close with a clunk but with a soft swishy noise like two fish colliding. Then she looks at her hand. It feels sticky. JW gets in beside his dad. He watches his dad insert the key. This should be good.

His dad starts the car and Booger does his best. The car shakes and a noise comes from up front that sounds like a cat is caught in the fan belt.

"I gotta get a tune-up," Dr. Martin says putting the car in reverse.

"Gotta have music," Georgia sings from the back.

JW turns on the radio at the same time as his dad applies the brakes. The result is about the same. Dr. Martin's foot goes right through the floorboards and the radio knob comes off in JW's hand.

"What the..." Dr. Martin tries to see his foot at the same time as Booger is pushing it back where it belongs. This time when Dr. Martin applies the brakes everything is fine. Sort of.

"JW, the radio."

JW puts the knob back on and turns it. This time music comes out of the speakers. It's supposed to be *A Shot of Rhythm and Blues* but it sounds more like *A Snot of Ribbons and Booze*.

"What is that? Try a different station."

Poor Booger, thinks JW, but he pushes the buttons. On comes Twist and Shout, then again it might be *Roll Over Beethoven* played backwards.

"Forget it."

"Use this." Paula hands JW her iPod. JW plugs it into the radio. There isn't a hole but Booger sucks it in.

The Black Eyed Peas start to play and they sound perfect. JW stares at the radio. It suddenly occurs to JW that he's still thinking of Booger as a Big Jellybean when in reality Booger is so much more.

He is miles smarter than JW and he is only days old. He can turn himself into anything, including things that run the way they're supposed to. He heals in hours. He can glide over sand carrying a gorilla. He can swim like a fish. He can communicate through his mind. He can play a CD he's never heard before.

You're something, Booger.

Thank you, mommy.

The Martin family has their own spot at Draper's Point. It's at the highest point of the park far above the Pacific Ocean. The parking lot is quite a way down near the observation level but if you know the secret way there is a back road that takes you to the top. As a result the Martins usually have it to themselves. Which is exactly what they want.

Georgia spreads out the blanket while Paula hands out the sandwiches and JW passes the juice boxes. They eat in silence enjoying the quiet and the view in equal measures. At last Dr. Martin clears his throat.

"First, I would like to thank the three of you for being so great the night the animals were let out. Because we stuck together and didn't panic it turned out to be something positive instead of the disaster it was intended to be. I want you to know I am very proud of you."

"Dad, you were the best."

"Thanks, Paula."

Dr. Martin takes the time to smile at each of his children.

"So we come here to Draper's Point when we have important things to say. I know I do and I think JW has as well. Georgia? Paula?"

Georgia straightens up.

"I miss mom."

"So do I," echoes Paula.

Dr. Martin takes his time replying.

"Your mother called today. She wanted to know if she could come back to the house."

"So what did you say?" Georgia asks staring at her dad.

"I said I wasn't ready for that. I said I thought she should have her own place in town and we'd go from there."

"And?"

"And she said I was always *so sensible.*"

The kids can feel the emotion in their dad's voice. But they also know he wasn't asking for their opinion he was just telling them what was going on.

"What about Yummy? We know you like her."

"I do like Yummy a lot. I enjoy her company. She makes me laugh."

"You and mom used to laugh all the time."

Dr. Martin is quiet. He knows they all remember how it was at the end. Laughter isn't what comes to mind.

"Love is based on trust. When trust is broken it's very difficult to mend. Like a glass you drop on the floor. You can glue the pieces back together but you're always waiting for it to break again...

"I love your mother but I'm not sure we can live together again."

21

Draper's Point Part Two

Time passes slowly sometimes. Other times it gallops along. This is one of the slow times.

"Well, JW," his dad says, "we could use some laughter and you're usually good for that."

"You're not referring to last time we were here, are you?"

"When you said to your mother, Mark Who?"

They all smile at this though it wasn't funny at the time.

"By the way, he apologized today. Said he made a big mistake and asked our forgiveness."

"Tell that to Janis Joplin!" This from Paula.

JW takes a deep breath.

"That's not what I want to talk about. What I want to talk about is my new friend."

"Niki, ooo la la," sings Georgia.

"Niki is ooo la la but that's not who I'm talking about."

The twins make faces.

"We'd know if you had another new friend," Georgia says.

"Want to bet?"

Suddenly the girls get it. "Big Pink!"

"Do you remember that piece of asteroid I bought?"

"The one that looked like a piece of old highway?"

"That one," JW says nodding.

"What did you do with it?" Georgia asks.

"Let's just say it ended up in the hot tub with a guinea hen egg."

"And you're going to tell us it hatched?"

"It did."

"No way!"

"Liar!"

"Do we have money where are mouths are?" JW is grinning at his twin sisters.

"Girls don't bet."

"You bet, you just never pay up!"

"That's our prerogative."

JW grins at his dad who can't figure out where JW is going with this.

"Okay, are you ready? And don't freak. This is my new friend, the best friend I'll ever have."

The other three stare at JW like he's crazy.

JW gets to his feet and stares at the Cherokee.

"Booger."

"Booger?"

"Nice name for a friend."

"Shhhhh... Booger, it's okay."

JW walks towards the car. The headlights flash.

"It's okay, Boog. Just be yourself. I want you to meet my family. *Our family.*"

The headlights flash again. Then the car melts and there stands Booger, the Giant Jellybean.

"Omigod!" Paula says for the hundredth time. "Omigod!"

"Omigod!" Georgia says for the hundredth-and-second time. "Omigod!"

"Omigod!" says Dr. Martin.

Dr. Martin doesn't really say Omigod! What Dr. Martin says is, "Howdy Booger."

It takes JW an hour to tell the story of Booger. His dad and his sisters listen fascinated as JW runs through the days. A lot has happened in two weeks. JW tells them about the broken beaker, waking up to Booger, Sheriff Riley and the bucking bronco bike, Mr. Walensky and the big poop, the basketball game, the fire at Devon Summer's house, Booger the Umbrella, swimming in Mark Nash's pool, the flying picnic table, dividing in Mr. Barber's class... everything but the fire at Crummie's. That's still a secret.

At first Booger sits on top of the picnic basket eating everything inside and the basket as well. It's hard work being a Cherokee. Then he slides in between the two girls and seems to go to sleep. They are enchanted with their new friend and quietly move their hands along his shiny silver skin. They listen as JW explains his worries about Inventors.

"But you'll be famous, JW!"

JW feels tears well up in his eyes. He shakes his head.

"You can't keep him a secret forever," Dr. Martin says.

"I know that. But if I tell anyone they'll take him away from me. They'll want to study him."

"Would that be so bad?"

"I keep seeing all those horrible FBI agents in E.T. All the white suits and the tubes and the plastic tunnel. I know how Elliott feels. He knows if those men take E.T., E.T. will die. That's how I feel about Booger. I don't want him to be a science experiment. I don't want him to die."

JW can't stop the flow now and soon everyone at the picnic has tears running down their cheeks.

"This is what he did when he was a bike. He likes to try things."
JW is saying this sideways because at this exact moment the Booger-
Cherokee is twice as long as Mark Nash, Famous Rock Star and
Reformed Rotten Person's stretch limousine. But only half as high.

"Hold on!"

The Cherokee is like a stretched elastic band and, yep, Booger
lets the back end go just as JW yells "Hold on!"

Whap! The back of the Cherokee takes off for the front. Whomp!
The rear bumper bounces off the front bumper.

"Hi, my name's Trunk, what's yours?"

"Oh hi, I'm Rad, I'm not sure we're supposed to be meeting like
this."

Five minutes later the Cherokee is back to normal but on a long hill
stuck behind a Recreational Vehicle. There is a sign on the back of
the RV that says *Road Roamers: Why Leave Home When You Can Take
It With You*? The oncoming lane is a steady stream of cars heading
back to the city.

For somebody who likes to be whipping along this is like being
a racehorse in a herd of cattle. But unlike normal vehicles which are
locked into specific shapes Booger decides the first thing he needs
to do is to see what is in front of this motorized snail.

He does this by inflating the tires until the Cherokee is sticking
up in the air five feet higher than the RV. There isn't one RV, there
are four of them! A Club of RVs and an overpass!

Georgia, who is bouncing back and forth between having the
time of her life and being utterly terrified — sometimes they're pretty
much the same thing — squeals, "We're a Monster Truck!"

Dr. Martin, who sees the overpass right in front of them, thinks
his last thought is going to be Duck!

But Booger sees the overpass too and brings the Cherokee down
just in time. This fright seems to anger Booger because, as soon as

they clear the bridge, Booger takes the Cherokee Monster Truck up and over the four *Why Bother Leaving Home When You Can Take Your House With You And Ruin Everybody Else's Day* Recreational Vehicles.

When JW comes down from the ceiling he looks back. The RVs seem to be okay. The lead driver is waving his arms and yelling at his passenger. JW turns back frontward and wishes he hadn't. There is a police car coming towards them and the driver has just turned on the siren and the flashing lights.

Oh man, Booger, you've done it this time!

"I imagine those flashing lights are for us," Dr. Martin says..

"I guess they didn't like us going *over* the RVs."

"All four of them."

"I liked it," Paula says.

"Serves 'em right," adds Georgia.

JW stares at his dad and they all start to laugh. Nobody is going to believe any of this. The police car slows down and pulls over onto the shoulder of the road. The Cherokee and the RVs go by going the other way. JW looks back and watches the cruiser do a u-turn.

"Here they come!"

"Maybe we should pull over?"

Booger speeds up instead pulling away from the Snails-on-Wheels. The police car has to wait until the RVs have room to pull over so it can pass. By the time the cruiser is clear Booger is a mile ahead.

"Hey Boog! You're about to be arrested. But don't worry, once you get settled we'll bring you a cake with a file in it."

The cop car is flying up behind them. Dr. Martin has sometime ago given up pretending he's driving the car.

"You'd better pull over Booger," he says.

But Booger has other ideas. Just as the cop car lands on their back bumper Booger slams on the brakes. The police have no choice but to ram the back of the Cherokee. And they would do except Booger inflates the tires just before they hit. The cruiser shoots underneath and out the front.

Booger comes down. The police car brake lights go on. Booger is going to ram the police cruiser except he has yet another idea. He reverses direction. One second JW is going fast forward, the next he's facing backwards. Booger is now heading right for the four RVs. Up and over goes the Cherokee but waiting on the other side is another police car with its lights and siren on.

Booger reverses direction again. Back over the four RVs he goes. Now the first police car is slowing down in front of them. The two policemen inside are probably thinking of getting out of the vehicle but before they can open their doors Booger lowers the Cherokee onto the cruiser and proceeds down the highway.

After that things are a bit up and down in the Cherokee. Paula and Georgia are now sitting on the trunk of the cruiser and JW and his dad are sitting on the hood. You can't see the cruiser but the shape is there and you can sort of hear the siren and the bottom of the Cherokee is flashing pink like that color you get when you put your hand over a flashlight.

"Booger, what are you going to do now?" JW asks. "I mean these guys will probably start shooting through the roof if you don't let them out of there."

"Ah oh!" This from Dr. Martin. JW looks out front. A third police car, lights flashing, is heading their way. JW looks back through the scrunched twins. The other police car is coming up the rear.

JW wants to help Booger but he can't see that Booger has any choice but to stop. There are police cruisers front and back and probably more coming. To the right are endless fields and to the left is a very steep drop with the Pacific Ocean at the bottom.

Stop Boog. We'll get out. When no one's looking turn into a backpack or something.

Booger ignores mommy and turns sharp left, cutting between two oncoming cars and heads down the steep hill. Yes, there is a guardrail. No, it doesn't stop Booger.

Down Booger goes.

Yes, there are big rocks. Yes, it's bumpy. Yes, Booger is going to prison for the rest of his life.

Halfway down, Booger releases the police car. JW, between bumps, can see the cruiser teetering on a large boulder. The policemen are trapped inside. The driver leans out his window his gun drawn. But there isn't much point in shooting, the Cherokee is heading for the ocean with nowhere else to go.

Georgia's last words are, "Can Booger float with us in here?"

JW's last words are, "I have no idea."

Dr. Martin's last words are, "He's managed everything else."

Paula's last words are "You're *so sensible*, dad."

A minute has passed. No one has drowned. No one is even wet. All four occupants of the car are sitting just as they were before they entered the Pacific Ocean. But they aren't under the Pacific Ocean, which is the big thing, they are in fact bobbing on top of it.

Paula is the first to speak. "Why is the outside of the car yellow?"

JW has a grin on his face and it's spreading.

"Booger's not actually a car anymore," JW says.

"If he's not the Cherokee, what is he?" Georgia wants to know.

Dr. Martin leans out the window, then leans out farther so he can look up. He pulls his head in and now he's grinning like a madman, too.

"Call me crazy — but I think we're in a Rubber Ducky."

"I am so, so, so *embarrassed*," Georgia says.

"This is beyond *embarrassed*," echoes Paula.

"We are landing at Crummie's in a Giant Rubber Ducky!"

"With a thousand people looking on!"

"Maybe a hundred," Dr. Martin says.

"That's more than enough to be embarrassed in front of."

"I'd say they looked pleased to see us."

"They're in hysterics."

"I would be too if I was on the beach looking at a Giant Rubber Ducky *farting* its way into shore."

"Why can't Booger be a cigarette boat or something?"

"The only thing he knows that floats is your rubber ducky in the bathtub."

"But does he have to keep blowing big bubbles out the back?"

"That's what's making us move."

"He could have a propeller."

"You explain it to him."

Any further discussion is cut off by the arrival of two police cruisers in Crummie's parking lot. Their sirens aren't on but the flashing lights are.

"Stay like this Booger," JW says. "If there's a time when no one's looking change into a picnic table."

Sheriff Riley arrives at the waterline at the same time as the Giant Rubber Ducky. Dr. Martin and the three kids hop out. The crowd cheers and gathers around the Ducky for a closer look.

"George, JW, can I talk to you for a moment?"

Dr. Martin and JW walk with Sheriff Riley away from the crowd.

"George, what can you tell me about a police cruiser being picked up by a Monster Cherokee on the PCH and then it was dropped off halfway down a hillside — it's still there by the way and isn't going anywhere till a crane arrives from the city." Sheriff Riley takes his hat off and scratches his head.

"But here's the part you'll like. Apparently the Monster Cherokee then drove into the Pacific Ocean where it changed into a..." —

Sheriff Riley can't keep a big smile from taking over his face — "...a Giant Rubber Ducky."

"That's quite a story," Dr. Martin says trying not to grin.

"Isn't it? You should hear it on the radio. We got officers radioing in from as far away as L.A. asking if they see a Giant Rubber Ducky should they pull it over? They want to know if *we consider it dangerous*? Could we describe it more fully? Would we say it was lemon yellow or school bus yellow? Here's my favorite: does it make a noise if you squeeze it?"

It's all Sheriff Riley can do not to burst out laughing.

"If it wasn't for the big yellow thing in front of me I'd be checking the two officers for drinking on duty."

"Did they get the license number of the Monster Cherokee?" JW asks.

"That's another odd thing. The license number they recorded was GRANITE which as we all know belongs to Jack Granite's black Mercedes. I sent an officer over there but neither Jack nor the car is there. Where's your car by the way?"

JW answers. "It's at home in the garage."

"You don't mind if I check?"

"No sir."

Sheriff Riley walks over to the other cruiser, talks to the men inside and they drive off. He comes back.

"So JW, tell me about this Giant Rubber Ducky."

"I'm going to get a coffee," Dr. Martin says. "You want one Jim?"

"Black with sugar, thanks... now JW, this wouldn't be another Inventors' project would it?"

"No sir. Dad and I got this idea at Halloween that if the pilgrims had landed on the West Coast instead of the East Coast, at Crummie's instead of Plymouth Rock, it might have looked something like this."

Sheriff Riley pauses. "You're puttin' me on."

"Yes sir. Can I tell you after Inventors?"

"You might as well. Once again, no one's going to believe me anyhow." Except maybe Special FBI Agent Angela Burns. She was going to love this.

The crowd drifts away its curiosity satisfied. Dr. Martin arrives with the coffees, milkshakes for JW and the twins and a laughing Yummy.

"I guess I'll have to keep the Giant Rubber Ducky as evidence," says Sheriff Riley thinking about the mountain of forms he'll have to fill in. Maybe he could get an early retirement package? But when he turns back to look at the evidence it isn't there. Just a picnic table. And it's not flying.

Sheriff Riley takes the lid off his coffee and blows on it.

"Well I'll be," is all he says.

22

Two Warnings

Jack Granite is sitting at one of the Crummie Burger picnic tables with Yummy Crummie. They are away from everyone else. Jack Granite is used to seeing the ocean from far above. It's different here with the waves crashing at his feet.

"It's nice here," he says at last. Yummy doesn't say anything. She doesn't know he tried to burn Crummie's down. She thinks there's a good person inside Jack Granite struggling to come out.

"I know you're never going to sell Crummie's to me," Jack Granite begins. "I didn't understand that at first. I thought you were just holding out for more money. But I get it now and I admire you for what you're doing here."

Jack Granite takes a deep breath. This part isn't easy.

"I've come to warn you about something. I've gotten involved with a very bad man. A truly *evil* man."

Jack Granite lets his words sink in.

"Last year I got in severe financial difficulties. I was in danger of losing everything. I was desperate and too proud of my reputation so I made a deal with this man. He bailed me out and he's been the one putting up the money to buy all this waterfront property. He's the one pushing me to get you to sell."

Jack Granite wants Yummy to like him but he's pretty sure it isn't going to end that way.

"I'm about to tell him that the deal is off. That I'm going to sell all the waterfront property and give him back his money plus interest. I'll probably have to sell Shipstead House to do it but that's okay too."

Jack Granite suddenly has a vision of himself living in one of the little fisherman's cottages right on the water. That would be okay.

"But this man won't be happy with getting his money back. He's going to want to keep going and I'm scared he'll try to force you to sell."

Jack Granite looks down.

"I'm worried about you and your daughter."

Yummy's heart twists in two.

"You think he'd hurt us?"

Jack Granite nods.

"We should go to the police," Yummy says.

"That will just make it worse. You'll spend the rest of your life in fear."

Yummy is angry now. "I've done nothing to deserve this!"

"I know. It's my fault. I'm truly sorry."

Yummy is on her feet now.

"So what do you suggest we do?"

"Take this." Jack Granite pushes a package across the table. "It's a letter detailing everything that's happened and a DVD of all my meetings with this man. There's enough here to keep him away. I'm going tonight to see this man and tell him that the deal's off. If I don't phone you by morning go to Sheriff Riley with Amanda, give him this package and ask for protection."

Yummy grabs the package, walks away and doesn't look back.

Special Agent Angela Burns stares out the window. If she looks far enough to the right she can see the sun rippling on San Francisco Bay. How did I end up with this job? she wonders. Special Agent in Charge of Unexplained Occurrences in California. Heck, she thinks, just about everything that happens in California is *Unexplained*.

Look at Los Angeles. Last week a man got into his car and disappeared. His wife was watching out the window. She says he got in the car, turned the key and that was it. Poof, he was gone.

I should go and turn that key, thinks Special Agent Angela Burns. Maybe I could disappear too.

She returns to her desk and spreads out the reports from Shipstead. There are six of them. She reads each one in turn. As she reads the last one, it's about a Jeep Cherokee that turns itself into a Giant Rubber Ducky, — *oh please, is everybody crazy but me?* — she circles a name with a red pen. She goes back through the other five reports and circles the same name five more times. She picks up the phone.

"Lawrence, I want you to go to Shipstead and find out everything you can about a fifteen-year-old boy named John Martin. And keep your eyes open for E.T. Do it now and don't lose the car."

Sheriff Riley is also thinking about John Martin. Special Agent Angela Burns may be a pain in the butt but he has to admit there have been some *seriously strange* things going on lately in quiet old Shipstead and all these strange things seem to have one common element, JW.

"BB!"

"Yes sir!"

"Get in here!"

BB's full name is Bunny Bunny Woods. Mrs. Woods told Mr. Woods that he could name the baby Bunny but that she had to have a middle name as well in case she didn't like her first name. Mr. Woods did what he was told, sort of. In the end he got an earful and the new baby got a nickname, BB. BB is twenty-seven, has dirty-blonde hair, blue eyes, is tall and skinny, and has a smile that could melt permafrost.

"BB."

"Yes, Sheriff Riley?"

Everybody else calls Sheriff Riley, Jim, but not BB.

"I want you to stake out Dr. Martin's place. Use your own car, no uniform. If you see anything *odd* let me know."

"What kind of *odd*, sir?"

"Anything out of the ordinary. Y'know like a Giant Rubber Ducky or…" Sheriff Riley starts to chuckle. He always thinks of BB as an *odd duck.*

"One of those landed at the beach at Crummie's," BB says.

"Yes BB. I was there, remember?"

"Oh, yes sir. You were the one that lost the evidence."

"Go BB! Go now! And don't let Dr. Martin see you. He won't like us spying on him."

"No sir. I mean, yes sir."

Jack Granite parks his Mercedes on the street. He hands the keys to Roman.

"They won't bother you out here. It's too visible."

Jack Granite can see Roman isn't convinced. Neither is Jack Granite.

"Lock the doors. There's a gun in the glove compartment. If I'm not out in an hour call the police and take off."

The two men shake hands.

"Good luck," Roman says meaning it.

"Thanks, I have a feeling I'm out of luck."

Lawrence Evans has been a FBI agent for seventeen weeks and three days. In that time the most exciting thing he's done is chase a suspected drug dealer. Unfortunately, the drug dealer escaped because Lawrence's shoelace came undone and he fell headfirst into a garbage can and when Lawrence ran limping back to his unmarked car it wasn't there. Some other crook had stolen it.

It wasn't a great beginning to his career and Lawrence is determined to do better this time. So far he's managed to ascertain that John Martin is actually called JW. That he lives with his father and sisters at 17 Grove St. He found all this out by looking in the phone book under Martin. There was a Dr. George and a Mildred. He'd phoned Mildred and asked for John.

"If you want JW look under Dr. George and if one of the girls answers tell her Miss Martin says hello. I taught them second grade. Goodbye."

Lawrence is now parked down the street from JW's house. He can't see the garage well but he has a clear view of the front door and the driveway. He's wearing black jeans, a black t-shirt and black sneakers, the ones without laces. He's pretending to be Mel Gibson in *Lethal Weapon*. He's kind of hoping the house will blow up and he'll capture the perpetrator. That would probably make up for tripping over his shoelace and losing the car.

It's nine o'clock. He'll wait until midnight then reconnoiter the place. It would be good if it didn't blow up then.

The door opens before Jack Granite can use the large brass knocker. He's been to this house before but never under these circumstances. The young bodyguard, Hans his name is, the one that shot the ball out of Mantis' mouth, leads him to the study. The man Jack Granite has come to see is sitting in his leather wheelchair smoking a cigar. The walls of the study are covered in photographs of dead animals, all shot by the Man in the Wheelchair.

Above the fireplace, the largest photograph shows a white rhinoceros lying on the ground a pool of blood around its head. What makes this photograph different from the others is the man sprawled in the dirt beside the dead rhino.

On Jack's first visit he made the mistake of asking about this photo.

"That's me in the dirt," the man had answered. "My back is broken. I keep it there to remind me."

Jack didn't ask what it reminded the man of. He didn't want to know.

"I gather there's something you wish to tell me?"

"Yes Max, there is. I've decided not to continue with the waterfront project. I'm selling all the property we have accumulated. I'll pay you back in full plus two million dollars for your trouble."

Max Keefer, The Man in the Wheelchair doesn't move. Jack Granite feels like he's staring at a cobra getting ready to strike.

"And this is all because Ms. Crummie won't sell her hamburger stand?"

"She doesn't have to sell her hamburger stand."

"I could make her sell it."

"No!"

The Man in the Wheelchair smiles.

"No!" repeats Jack Granite. "You will not hurt her in any way. I have documented everything. I've recorded every conversation we've ever had!"

"I don't believe you."

Jack Granite extends his hand. On his wrist is a large Rolex watch. Jack Granite pushes a button on the side and the watch face turns into a miniature television screen. The man's face appears. "I don't believe you," it says.

Now Max Keefer isn't smiling.

"And where are these recordings?"

"In a safe place. If I'm not back in my car by ten o'clock a letter and a video of our conversations will be given to the police."

The Man in the Wheelchair looks at his own watch.

"It's only nine-twenty. We still have forty minutes to enjoy ourselves. Do you like baseball?"

BB parks her cruiser on Grand and hikes over to Grove St. to check things out. In her head she calls it a stroll-by. She's wearing jeans, a sweatshirt that says Space Cadet and a Mighty Ducks' baseball hat. This is BB's idea of going undercover.

As she approaches 17 Grove St. she hears music. There's a light on in the garage and the first thing she sees is a gorilla dancing. That's definitely out of the ordinary. She gallops back to Grand and phones in.

"Sheriff Riley?"

"Go ahead, BB."

"There's a gorilla dancing in the garage."

BB is waiting for a reply but all she hears is a sigh. A big one.

"That's okay BB. The gorilla lives there. His name is Mick. He likes to dance."

"So none of that is odd?"

"It's *odd* but not what we're looking for. Try again."

"Can you imagine what it's like to be a full, vigorous man and suddenly be reduced to this?" Max Keefer studies Jack Granite's face. He knows Jack is afraid but he admires the way Jack is standing up to his fear. The Man in the Wheelchair lets the silence build. They're in the laundry room in the basement now. The young bodyguard, Hans, comes through the door carrying two baseball bats. He throws one to his friend Joe and waits.

"There is one thing," Jack says at last. He has one more card, he might as well play it.

"Yes Jack?"

"On Halloween night I tried to set fire to Crummie's."

"Really, Jack? How enterprising of you."

"Before I could get it going a boy smelt the gasoline and yelled at me. I had to run for it."

"Not something I could do Jack."

Now the huge amount of fear that Jack has been hiding in his brain floods into his body.

"Why are you telling me this, Jack?"

"I was running towards my car, way ahead of the boy, when suddenly something caught up to me."

"Something, Jack?"

"It… it looked like a giant jellybean."

The two young bodyguards laugh. Max Keefer shakes his head.

"It was Halloween, Jack."

"I know that but this thing didn't have legs and it caught up to me like I was standing still."

And you were running like a scared rabbit thinks the Man in the Wheelchair. Jack Granite, famous astronaut, caught setting fire to a hamburger stand.

Max Keefer looks down at his watch.

"That's very interesting Jack. So you think this 'jellybean' was some being from outer space? And you're telling me in case I'm willing to trade this information for all the aggravation you've caused me?"

Now the Man in the Wheelchair can see fear on Jack Granite's face. Good. He likes fear on other people's faces. Still Jack's little Halloween story is intriguing. Jack isn't the kind to make things up. Max Keefer smiles. To be the first man to hunt and kill an Alien Being would put his name in the history books forever.

"I don't suppose you know the boy's name?"

"John Martin."

Roman looks at the clock in the Mercedes for the hundredth time. One more minute and he calls the cops and takes off. He doesn't want to abandon Mr. Granite but there is no way he's going into that house to rescue him. He'll never be that brave.

Roman watches as the gates at the end of the driveway swing open. Two burly men come through the gates carrying a man between them. It's Jack Granite and he's in bad shape. His legs are dragging behind him. His head is down and Roman can see blood spilling out of his employer's nose onto the driveway.

The two men let go. Jack Granite drops to the pavement and doesn't move. One of the men turns back but the other comes over to Roman's side of the car. Roman has the doors locked. He puts the window down an inch so he can hear what the man is saying.

"A hospital would be a good idea. 'Night."

BB doesn't have a clue what she's looking for. If a gorilla dancing in the garage isn't *odd*, what is? She strolls by 17 Grove St. again. This time the gorilla is sitting in a hanging seat. He waves to BB. She waves back. Nothing about the house seems odd but the young man slouched down in the car across the street seems *suspicious*. Maybe that counts.

BB decides to walk around the block and come at the house from the back. This is not a good idea but she doesn't know that.

JW arrives home from Niki's riding Bicycle Booger. As he swings into the driveway Booger changes into a tricycle. JW laughs as his feet hit the pavement.

Very funny, Boog.

I thought so.

What do you say we sit in the hot tub?

We could invite Eric and Gerry.

We'll have a party.

JW shuts the garage door, says goodnight to Mick and Stevie, and heads into the house to find Eric and Gerry.

Roman looks up at the doctor. She's his age and pretty.

"Are you Mr. Granite's son?"

"No, I work for him."

"Does he have family?"

"I don't know. He's never talked about anyone."

"Then I guess I'll tell you what's happened."

Roman nods.

"He's been badly beaten, but I guess you know that?"

Roman nods again.

"Both legs are broken. I imagine they've been hit with something heavy like a baseball bat. His stomach area is covered in round burns like a cigar would make. He has two cracked ribs. His nose is broken. I am required by law to tell the police about this but Mr. Granite is begging me not to. He says it was an accident. He says if I tell the police every reporter in California will be here by morning. He's probably right about that."

The pretty doctor looks at Roman.

"Was it an accident?"

"Yes."

"Okay," the doctor says turning to go. She turns back. "Two more things. Mr. Granite wants you to phone Yummy, have I got the name right?"

Roman nods.

"Call Yummy and tell her everything is alright, not to worry."

Roman nods again.

"Next, Mr. Granite is missing his false teeth."

"False teeth?"

"They're missing. You should bring another pair. He's having trouble talking."

BB is having trouble figuring out which house is behind Dr. Martin's. She finally thinks to look up and right away spies the tree that sticks out of Dr. Martin's garage. There's some fuzzy ball at the top that looks like a sleeping monkey. If a gorilla dancing *isn't out of the ordinary,* a monkey in a tree sticking out of a garage probably isn't either.

She cuts between two houses and climbs over a fence. Now she's in Dr. Martin's backyard crouching behind a big log. She hears a boy laughing and watches him climb into the hot tub carrying a hockey stick, a bottle of pop and a bag of chips. Suddenly BB is hungry too.

Next she sees a huge snake lift its head above the side of the hot tub. The snake checks things out then slithers into the bubbling water. I guess that's not *odd* either, thinks BB feeling she's getting the hang of this.

Then the boy yells "Jump Eric!" and BB looks up in time to see a baboon, this one has a bright-blue butt, standing in a second floor window. The baboon leaps into space and lands in the hot tub with a mighty splash!

Now the boy is laughing again and BB wants to laugh too. This place is better than an amusement park. BB watches as the blue-butted baboon dances in the middle of the hot tub and then the two large snakes are dancing too.

Two large snakes? thinks BB. Where did the second snake come from? BB doesn't think to miss the hockey stick. Then she stops thinking because the log she's leaning on suddenly looks at her. It has big eyes with a big mouth underneath.

ZZ Top yawns. Who's having a party?

"Yummy? You don't know me. My name's Roman. I work for Jack Granite. He says to tell you everything's okay. You're not to worry... He's in the hospital. He's pretty beaten up. But he's going to be okay."

"That you, Sheriff?"

"Yes, BB. What have you got?"

"That place is full of weird animals."

"Yes it is, BB."

"Most of them are in the hot tub at the moment."

Sheriff Riley chuckles at this.

"There's even a big lizard thing. I thought it was a log. I was leaning on it."

"Are you okay?"

"I'm fine. The lizard was friendly. Reminds me of my first boyfriend. Alfred. Moved to Alaska. Sells swimming pools."

Sheriff Riley tries to picture this.

"So is that it, BB?"

"Yes sir, except…"

"Except what, BB?"

"Except there's a young man sitting in a car on Grove St. watching Dr. Martin's house."

"Did you get the license plate number BB?"

"Yes, I did."

"Good work, BB. What is it?"

Manfred Mann is trying to sleep without much success. Too much noise.

"JW's having a party," Manfred says.

"You don't say," Mann replies.

"Eric's there and Gerry and the new guy too, I think."

"Perhaps we should join them?"

"I imagine by the time we got there, the party would be over."

"I imagine you're right."

"Night, Mann."

"Night, Manfred."

⅋

Lawrence Evans, brand-new FBI agent, opens his car door. It's not midnight but he can't stand it any longer. Ever since he observed JW's bike change from a bicycle to a tricycle he's been dying to check it out.

He shuts the door softly and looks around. Everything seems quiet on the street except for the faint sound of laughter and music coming from the suspect's backyard. Lawrence walks up the driveway. He's not too worried about being caught. He's got his gun and FBI badge.

He opens the side door of the garage and disappears inside.

Every month some salesman is trying to sell Dr. Martin a security system and every month he tells the salesman he already has one.

"No you don't."

"Try to break in."

Lawrence Evans, brand-new FBI agent, waits for his eyes to adjust to the dark interior of the garage. The suspect's bike must be here somewhere. He takes two steps forward and is suddenly spun around. A huge hairy arm wraps around his neck forcing him back against iron bars. Before he can draw his gun another hairy arm has snatched it and his FBI badge.

"FBI! Let me go!"

The hairy arm doesn't let go. Lawrence tries again.

"FBI! Let me go!"

Sheriff Riley pulls his cruiser up behind the unmarked car. He's angry. The FBI staking out Dr. Martin's house without asking him or at least telling him shows a total lack of respect. He slams the door of the cruiser. He's of a mind to tell Dr. Martin. Maybe George can sue them for harassment or something.

The unmarked car is empty. Sheriff Riley walks up the driveway.

The agent must be here somewhere. Then he hears a voice coming from the garage.

"Please, let me go!"

Sheriff Riley opens the garage door and flicks on the light. Mick has the young agent pinned against the bars of his cage. The agent has his two hands on the gorilla's arm trying to pull it off but it would take five agents to do that. More of a worry is the gun Mick is waving around.

"Mick, how's it going?" Sheriff Riley reaches in and Mick hands him the gun and FBI badge.

"Sheriff! Am I glad to see you. I'm Agent Lawrence Evans. I'm with the FBI."

Sheriff Riley studies Lawrence as he takes the bullets out of the gun and puts them in his pocket.

"It's a good thing you wore black pants, isn't it Agent Lawrence?"

Lawrence tries to laugh. "I got a bit nervous when the gorilla was waving the gun around."

"It's your gun, isn't it?"

"Yes sir, it's my gun."

"Does Dr. Martin know you're here?"

"No, sir. But maybe you didn't hear me. I'm with the F... B... I."

"My hearing's good. Do you have a search warrant?"

"No. I didn't think..."

"Stop right there, son. You finally said something that makes sense."

"Sheriff? Where are you going? Please make the..."

Sheriff Riley doesn't hear the rest. He walks across the street to Agent Lawrence's unmarked car and puts the gun and badge in the glove compartment. Then he goes to his cruiser and picks up his phone.

"Steve? It's Jim. I got a car on Grove St. needs towing. It's the black car across from Dr. Martin's place. I want you to take it to the airport in San Francisco and leave it in long-term parking. Thanks."

Sheriff Riley hangs up and punches in a new number.

"BB? I want you to get your uniform on, pick up Robbie and bring a cruiser over to Dr. Martin's house. Mick, the gorilla, has caught a burglar. He's holding him in the garage. The guy's an FBI agent but make like you don't believe him. Let him go in the morning. I'll be at home if you need me."

Sheriff Riley walks into the backyard. "Hey JW. Beautiful night for a party."

"Yes, sir. You're welcome to join us."

"I wouldn't mind sitting for a minute. Stars look good from here."

"Can I get you something?"

"No, I'm fine, thanks. Where's Gerry?"

"He's here somewhere. The hot water makes him sleepy."

Stay with Gerry, Boog.

Yes, mommy.

"I need to warn you about something, JW."

JW's heart flips.

"As you know there have been some strange doings in Shipstead lately. The FBI has got interested in all this strangeness. And guess whose name keeps popping up?"

"Mine?"

"Bingo."

"No, listen, you don't understand. I'm Agent Lawrence. I'm with the F.B.I."

"Prove it," BB says putting the handcuffs on.

"The Sheriff took my badge."

"You said the gorilla took it."

"He took it first. The Sheriff took it from the gorilla."

"Robbie, you seen the Sheriff?"

"Not for days."

"Me neither."

"Okay, okay. My wallet's in my car. My FBI photo ID is there."

"What car are you talking about?"

"The one across the street."

BB escorts her prisoner down the driveway. There isn't any car across the street. Like a nightmare Agent Lawrence's future passes before his eyes. For the rest of his days he'll be called No-Car Lawrence. He looks over at BB.

"I don't suppose you guys are hiring?"

23

The Monster
from the Lost Lagoon

JW finishes his chores at *The Pet Vet* and rides Bicycle Booger over to Crummie's. He nearly runs into Niki coming around the corner. She's carrying a tray full of drinks and looks stressed but she's glad to see him.

"Hey JW, hey Boog. You were very funny last night Booger." Niki gives JW a kiss and disappears. The night before, Niki, JW and Booger, watched *The Monster from the Lost Lagoon* over at Niki's house. Niki's mom was out so they'd had the house to themselves.

At first Booger was content to watch the movie sitting on the couch and eating popcorn out of a bowl on the floor but then he got bored with this and started copying all the actors in the movie. When the Monster from the Lost Lagoon finally appeared Booger decided it would be much more fun to become the scary Monster and terrorize Niki and Mommy.

"Booger! We can't see the movie!" Booger the Monster was so big he filled the room. JW felt like he was drowning in blue Jello.

"Thank you."

Then Booger hid behind the couch and every time the movie got scary he would bring cold slimy tentacles up and over the back of the sofa.

"Can you imagine taking Booger to a theater?"

Booger didn't know what a theater was but JW's question made Niki laugh so Booger was pleased.

JW sits down with Miguel and Ty. His shiny black bike he keeps right beside him.

"Ach JW," Ty says. "Are the wee critters all fed an' accounted for?"

JW is dying to tell his friends about Booger scaring the poop out of Snuffy the Yapper by suddenly becoming the Monster from the Lost Lagoon but he thinks better of it.

"It's not the same without Janis."

"You old hag," squawks Miguel.

The boys are quiet for a moment. Everybody misses Janis. Niki arrives with four burgers, four fries and four milkshakes. The boys expect her to sit down but she turns and is gone.

"What about your burger?" Miguel shouts.

"It's not mine," yells back Niki doing a pirouette. Miguel and Ty look at JW.

"Tell me Big Pink is joinin' us and I'll be a happy man."

"You're always happy Ty, with or without Big Pink."

"That's true JW, but I could be happier."

JW knows what Niki's doing. She's nudging him to tell Miguel and Ty about Booger. But if he tells them they won't be able to keep it a secret. But Sheriff Riley says the FBI is interested in him. And tomorrow is Inventors and JW still isn't sure what he's going to do. Maybe Miguel and Ty could help with that.

"And JW, Inventors is tomorrow. Have you created your little mun from another planet yet?" Ty asks putting his hands up beside his ears and wiggling his fingers.

JW gives Miguel a dirty look.

"He forced it out of me!"

"Aye. I had to promise to go with him to 'the Wicked Witch's."

"A fate worse than death."

Ty bends over looking under the picnic table.

"JW, what have you done with the extra burger and fries?"

JW puts his hands up to his ears and wiggles his fingers.

"My little mun from another planet just ate them."

A silver Rolls Royce pulls into the parking lot at Crummie's. The license plate spells RHINO. Inside, the Man in the Wheelchair splits an apple in two with his bare hands. The young man opposite him watches the older man's arm muscles ripple under his shirt. His legs may be useless, thinks the young man, but those hands could rip your heart out. The young man points at JW.

"He's the blond kid sitting with the other two at the picnic table. He rode his bike here from his dad's clinic. His dad's a vet."

The Man in the Wheelchair stares at the young man sitting opposite him. He must be very nervous but he's not showing it.

"Mr. Skinulis, you already told me that."

"Yes, sir."

"I want you to go over to the boys and pretend to be a reporter."

"Okay."

"Take the recorder beside you and tell the boys you want to interview them."

"What about?"

The Man in the Wheelchair frowns. He doesn't like to be interrupted.

"Perhaps, Mr. Skinulis, you could inquire why this hamburger place has such a revolting name but is obviously popular in spite of it?"

Or because of it, thinks the young man but he decides not to say this. He decides to be quiet. Maybe that will work better. This Max guy is truly scary.

"The important thing is that the boys each go away with one of these pens. They have a microphone inside. I wish to hear their conversation for the next few hours."

The young man picks up one of the pens. It's black with *People Magazine* written in white on the side. "Okay, I'll try. After that everything's cool, right? I won't owe you anything?"

"Yes Mr. Skinulis. If I find out what I want to know everything's, as you say, cool."

JW's enjoying himself. Miguel and Ty have been pushing their bikes for a couple of minutes now and JW is still wheeling around like he doesn't even know he's going UPhill.

"Ach JW, are you wearing rocket-powered sneakers or something?"

"It's that new bike," Miguel says.

"JW, if you've invented a bike that will go uphill you'll be a gazillionaire."

JW rides back to his friends. He's made a decision.

"Let's go over to Dead Man's Lookout. There's something I want to show you."

It's that time between day and night when everything blends together. The low streetlights are on in the park but they're not doing much yet. The sun is setting over the Pacific like a ball of fire sinking into the blue water. There are a few people around but JW steers the boys to a part of the park that seems deserted.

"Here you try it." JW gets off Bicycle Booger and trades bikes with Ty. "Whatever you do don't turn the handlebars." JW laughs inside at this. If there's one thing you can count on it's that Ty will do the thing he's been told not to.

Sure enough. Ty hasn't gone thirty feet before he twists the right handlebar and Booger changes the back wheel from normal to GIANT size.

"Whoa!" Ty screams. Booger flips over but manages to deposit Ty on the ground without breaking anything. Ty looks up at his friends grinning.

"JW, I'm lovin' this!" Ty spies the pen the reporter has given him lying in the grass and clips it back onto his shirt. His mum will want to hear all about his interview with the guy from *People Magazine*.

Ty climbs back on Bicycle Booger and heads back down the path. This time he turns the left handlebar but gently. Booger deflates the front tire. Ty turns the right handlebar and the back tire deflates. Ty is riding a mini-bike. Then he twists both handlebars the other way and both tires grow until Ty is six feet up on a MONSTER BIKE.

Once again it's The Bicycle Booger Rodeo Show brought to you by the friendly folks from Planet X. Planet X is what JW is thinking about as his friends turn Booger into a bucking bronco. Where is Booger from? JW tries to picture a whole planet of Boogers. It *boogers the mind* is his last thought on the matter.

Miguel has a turn. Then Ty, then Miguel again, then JW. They're so intent on watching each other that they don't notice the silver Rolls Royce parked behind the trees. Or the men spying on them. Finally all three boys are sprawled on the grass laughing, content to watch the sun disappear for another day.

The Man in the Wheelchair rips another apple in half. He has to admit young Mr. Skinulis did a good job. Telling the boys he was working on a list of the ten best hamburger joints in America was inspired. Did the boys think Crummie's should be on the list? Number One on the list is what the boys thought. The Man in the Wheelchair thinks there might be a fortune to be made in franchising Crummie's but that's for another day. Right now he's hunting game and the game is the biggest trophy of all time.

"So, JW" Ty says over the speaker in the silver Rolls Royce. "Would this bike be your Inventors project?"

"It's not a bike."

"If it's not a bike what is it?"

"What do you want it to be?"

"Big Pink."

"Shut your eyes."

The Man in the Wheelchair watches through his binoculars as Booger changes from a bicycle into a full-sized Barbie Doll.

"Okay, now look."

For once Ty and Miguel are speechless.

Max Keefer and his two bodyguards listen to JW telling his friends about Booger, the alien being born in his hot tub. *Booger*, another unsuitable name, thinks the Man in the Wheelchair, but that's easily remedied. Now the question is what will it take to get this *Booger* away from its owner. Money? Probably not. Still one must try.

JW sees the silver Rolls Royce gliding towards them. "Be a bike, Booger, hurry!"

The three boys watch as the Rolls cuts across the grass and stops sideways about twenty feet away. A tough looking guy gets out of the front passenger seat carrying a briefcase. He walks towards the three boys and stops in front of JW.

"My boss would like to buy your bike."

Before JW can answer the tough guy opens the briefcase. It's full of money, in neat rows. This is right out of the movies thinks JW.

"Sorry, it's not for sale."

"Mine is," says Ty.

"How much is in there?" asks Miguel his eyes wide.

"Two hundred thousand."

Miguel and Ty stare at JW. Two hundred thousand! JW picks up Bicycle Booger. "C'mon guys, let's get out of here."

"Stay where you are."

Now the tough looking guy has a gun in his other hand. It's

aimed at Ty's heart. The driver of the Rolls gets out of the car and walks over beside the tough looking guy.

"Grab the bike, the shiny black one."

Everyone stands still. JW doesn't believe the guy would shoot three kids in a park but still... The driver pushes the bike over to the Rolls, opens the back door and lifts the bike inside.

"Lie down," the guy with the gun orders.

JW doesn't want to lie down but the tough guy takes a step towards Ty. His gun isn't three feet from Ty's brain. JW lies down and Miguel and Ty follow.

"Stay there."

As soon as the Rolls is on the paved road heading out of the park the three boys are on their feet.

"C'mon! We've got to get the license number." JW picks up Miguel's bike. He stands up and Miguel hops on the seat. Ty is already heading for the roadway.

"Got your phone?" JW shouts at Miguel.

"Yeah!"

"Call Sheriff Riley. Tell him what's happened."

"Not about Booger?"

"Tell him they stole my special bike. He'll understand."

It's hopeless, all the boys can see that. The Rolls is way too far ahead. The only good thing is the car has turned left on Harper and that's downhill!

"He's not there. They're paging him."

"Call Crummie's. Tell Niki to get the license number as it goes by!"

Max Keefer, The Man in the Wheelchair, puts his hand on the shiny black bike. Amazing. It feels like metal. A bit sticky. He moves his hand to the tire. Feels like rubber. If he hadn't seen the *Booger* change shapes with his own eyes he wouldn't believe any of this.

"It seems we owe Mr. Granite an apology."

Hans and Joe, sitting in the front, laugh. Hans looks back at his boss.

"What are you going to do with that thing?"

Max Keefer strokes the bike like it was a dog or a cat.

"I haven't decided yet."

"I wonder what it really looks like?" Joe the driver asks.

"That's very perceptive of you Joe. I was just wondering the same thing. Perhaps one of Han's cigarettes would convince our new friend to show us who he really is."

Hans lights a cigarette and reaches back to hand it to his boss but because the bike is between them he can't quite reach.

"Your lighter will be sufficient."

Hans throws his lighter to the Man in the Wheelchair and watches as his boss lights it, then grins as his boss adjusts the flame to its maximum. The lighter hisses like a blowtorch. This should be good, thinks Hans. I wonder if the weird thing can scream.

Then Hans makes a mistake.

A Big One.

The silver Rolls shouldn't be going west on Harper it should be going east towards the PCH. Joe, the driver, has also made a mistake.

Joe looks in his rearview mirror curious to see what affect the three-inch flame is going to have on the weird thing in the back. In the distance he can see two bikes turn onto Harper. There are two riders on the one bike so it's definitely the boys. And it's downhill and the boys are gathering speed. Joe pushes a button under the dash and the rear license plate flips over. Now instead of RHINO it says JOKER, a registration that leads to a dummy company in Vegas.

Joe looks ahead. The traffic light turns yellow. He puts his foot down and the silver Rolls accelerates. No way he's waiting for a red light.

At the same time Hans pushes the button to lower his window.

The boys are flying.

"I've never gone this fast before!" Miguel shouts holding on for dear life. It's Miguel's bike but JW is upfront steering.

"We're gaining!"

"We need a red light!"

Miguel means he wants the Rolls to be stuck at a red light but exactly the opposite happens. In the distance they see the silver car run a yellow light while in front of them the traffic light turns red.

"Hang on!"

"No more stepmother!" Miguel yells.

"YYYYYYEEEEEEAAAAAAAA!" scream the three boys together. The traffic starts forward but JW and Ty keep going steering for the middle of the intersection. JW and Miguel fly through but Ty isn't quite as lucky. A red Honda Civic clips Ty's back tire sending him careening into the curb and up onto the sidewalk where he nearly collides with old Mrs. Johnson walking her mother.

"Watch where you're going young man!"

"Sorry ma'am. They've stolen our Alien Being. We're trying to get him back!"

"Then don't dillydally!"

"Yes ma'am!"

JW looks back. Ty waves. He's alright. Keep going!

Then it happens. The Man in the Wheelchair brings the lighter down to scare Booger.

Joe's eyes are glued to the rearview mirror. He wants to see what the bike changes into.

Hans lowers his window to throw the cigarette out. He's not allowed to smoke in the car.

That's what a VERY ANGRY BOOGER has been waiting for. In

a flash Booger shoots out the window and rears up in front of the silver Rolls Royce.

At this particular moment there are probably two hundred people in the vicinity, either in cars or walking the sidewalks of Harper Avenue and it's safe to say that of the two hundred people not one is prepared for what happens next. For suddenly The Monster from the Lost Lagoon fills Harper Avenue. Thirty feet wide and a hundred feet high the GIANT MONSTER dives towards the windshield of the silver Rolls Royce.

"What the!" Joe screams slamming on the brakes and turning the wheel hard to the right. The Rolls bangs up onto the sidewalk smashing hard into the corner of Sproules Drug Store. There's a shower of glass and wood. The radiator bursts filling the street with steam and a geyser of hot water. The car horn begins blaring on and off.

"Did you see that!" Miguel shouts. "Wow!"

"That was Booger!"

The boys arrive at the accident. Joe and Hans are both wrestling with air bags.

"Booger!"

JW's shiny black bike appears from the other side of the Rolls.

"Way to go Boog! You showed'em!"

"Let's get out of here before the cops show up," Ty says. Miguel's phone rings. He hands it to JW.

"It's Sheriff Riley."

"Hi Sheriff. I… I was calling to tell you there's been an accident on Harper. Just happened. A Rolls Royce just ran into Sproules… Yeah, I've got my bike back. Everything's okay."

But it isn't. Suddenly the back door of the silver Rolls swings open and out crawls the scariest man JW has ever seen. He slithers out on to the sidewalk like a deadly snake. The man's shoulder is on fire. He rolls and the fire goes out but his jacket keeps smoking. The Man in the Wheelchair stares up at JW and his face curls into a look of pure hatred.

"Let's get out of here!" Ty says grabbing JW's t-shirt. The sound of sirens is coming from all directions.

JW doesn't need to be told twice. He hops on Bicycle Booger and the three boys head for Crummie's to tell Niki what just happened.

24

Inventors

Inventors is an old tradition in Shipstead, California. It dates back to the day, over a century ago, when young Tom Dickenberry — sitting on the dock near where Crummie's is now — invented the telephone. He was a mechanic by trade and his girlfriend Ivy had just taken a job in New York City. Tom needed a telephone so he could talk to Ivy.

A week later he read how Alexander Graham Bell had scooped his idea. He wrote to Ivy in New York, "Boy, when you invent something you'd better not dawdle or it will be somebody else's invention. These things are in the air."

Tom Dickenberry never left Shipstead and Ivy never left New York and they never talked on Tom's telephone but none of that stopped Tom from starting the Inventors' Club and out of that grew the annual competition to find the best new student invention in Shipstead. So instead of Science Fair, Shipstead has Inventors, all of which tickles the fancy of the Shipstead townsfolk because if they'd wanted to be like everybody else they wouldn't live in Shipstead.

So there.

Inventors in Shipstead is always held on the first Sunday in November, in the afternoon. For the last few years it's been held outdoors in Granite Park. This park, like the high school, was donated by Jack Granite when he developed the land around it. At the entrance is a statue of a smiling Jack Granite in his astronaut's suit holding his helmet in the crook of his arm. Quite often there's a seagull standing on Jack Granite's head enjoying the view.

Each year Jack Granite has a stage set up near the statue. Each year Jack Granite donates a first prize of one thousand dollars to be given to the student judged to have the best invention.

Unlike most Science Fairs the winner of Inventors is not chosen by a panel of judges but rather by the applause of the crowd. And there is always a good crowd on hand because this is Shipstead and the townsfolk like to support anything close to home.

JW rides Bicycle Booger into the park and surveys the scene. The place is packed but amid the people JW recognizes some of last's year's contestants and over by the stage he can see Gloria and Dougie their heads together talking.

JW's dad spots him and comes over. He has Ringo on a leash and Yummy is beside him with Amanda and Eddie.

"Hey, JW. Have you figured out what you're going to do?"

JW shakes his head. "Only what I'm *not* going to do."

"You're going to have to do it sometime."

"I'm working on that."

Yummy laughs. "So, are you two boys going to let the girls in on this or is it a secret?"

"Secret."

"Don't tell us then. Amanda and I can't keep secrets, can we sweetheart?"

"I just can't keep them." Amanda says.

JW is so nervous his palms are sweating and his heart is racing. Sheriff Riley had called an hour ago.

"JW, you know that accident you phoned me about?"

"Yes sir."

"Do you know who that was in the car?"

"No sir."

"That was Max Keefer, better known as Rhino. He's the biggest loan shark on the West Coast."

JW didn't know what to say.

"He's very very bad news, JW. He's definitely not someone you want to mess with."

JW remembers the scariest man he's ever seen crawling out of his car like a snake. Then the look on his face when he saw JW standing there.

"Is there anything you want to tell me, JW?"

"No sir."

"Maybe after Inventors?"

"Maybe."

JW's already made his mind up not to betray Booger, the trouble is, between Max Keefer and the FBI, he and Booger are going to have to do something drastic. In the meantime, JW's name is still on the list of contestants. In fact, his is the last name, and he still has no idea what he's going to do. He does think he might get away with a bicycle that can change tire sizes but he knows afterwards he and Booger are going to have to disappear and fast.

He'll think of something.

"Ladies and Gentlemen, thank you all for coming. It's gratifying in an age when athletics are seemingly valued more than academics to see so much support for Inventors. Thank you." Mr. Barber, JW's biology teacher, is this year's Master of Ceremonies.

"Before we look at this year's inventions, and I can tell you there are some great ones, I'd like to invite Jack Granite to come on stage. As most of you know Mr. Granite not only donates the first prize of a thousand dollars but he also has his construction company put up this stage for us every year. We're lucky to have such a civic-minded person as Jack Granite living in our town."

Roman pushes Jack Granite on stage. Jack is seated in a wheel-chair, both legs in casts, bandages across his nose. In his hand he holds a long metal flagpole flying the flag of the United Nations. As the crowd applauds enthusiastically he takes the microphone from Mr. Barber.

"Thank you. If I told you I fell off my skateboard would you believe me?"

The crowd laughs.

"I consider it a real privilege to be involved in Inventors. I like things that encourage kids to be creative, to think for themselves.

"This year, as most of you know, marks the 40th anniversary of Man's first landing on the moon. On that historic day 40 years ago Neil Armstrong planted the Stars and Stripes on the surface of the moon for all the world to see. I like to think that was the day the American way of life took precedence over all others.

"Later today, I will be flying to Cape Canaveral to be on hand for tomorrow's scheduled shuttle launch. Two days from now Denise Franklin will land on the moon and plant the flag of the United Nations, beside the American flag that Neil Armstrong left so many years before.

"As a special treat I talked NASA into sending me the actual flag that will be going to the moon."

Jack Granite holds the United Nations' flag aloft.

"I thought it would be fun to pass it around so that everyone here will know their fingerprints are on the moon."

Jack Granite passes the flag to a young girl in the front row while everybody cheers.

"We've come a remarkably long way in a remarkably short time. As a nation we should be very proud.

"We should also be very proud of the young people we see before us today. I've had the rare privilege of *traveling* among the stars. With the help of these future inventors, someday we will *live* among the stars. Thank you."

"Our first Inventors' contestant is Angela Hopkins. Angela please come up and tell us about your project."

Angela is in Georgia's class at Shipstead High. She bounces up on stage dragging her beagle Chuck behind her. Mr. Barber hands her the microphone.

"Hi. I've invented a water bottle with two ends so that when you go for a walk with your favorite dog you can both have a drink."

Angela takes a drink, then holds the bottle down so Chuck can put his mouth around the bottom straw. Angela squeezes and Chuck coughs. Most of the water seems to end up on the stage. Everyone laughs including Angela.

"Thank you Angela," says Mr. Barber. "Our next presenter is Peter Ritson."

JW doesn't recognize Peter, which means he probably goes to Granite. He comes on stage dragging a garden hose.

"Thanks Mr. Barber. I've invented a two-handled car brush so that you can wash the car in half the time."

Someone turns the water on and yep, water comes out of both brushes. Everybody cheers as Peter demonstrates how to wash a pretend car with both hands at the same time. The way Peter does it like a dance makes it pretty funny.

"OR, you can wash two cars at the same time!"

If the first demonstration was humorous this one is hilarious. At one point Peter has one brush fully extended over the hood of one car while the other brush is fully extended in the opposite direction. This second brush is supposed to be washing the hubcap of the other car but all it's doing at the moment is pouring water into Peter's sneaker.

Mr. Barber comes on stage shaking his head. There is water everywhere.

"Thank you, Peter. Our next participant is Melanie Patterson.

Melanie, what have you got for us and I hope it doesn't involve water."

Melanie is about twelve with long blond hair which she wears in a braid down her back. She comes on stage with two girlfriends carrying tree branches.

"Hi. I've made a solar-powered skipping rope. This is for when you're by yourself with no one to turn the rope. You just need two trees or poles and the sun does the rest."

Melanie's skipping rope looks like any skipping rope except, instead of handles, each end is attached to a small black box which in turn is attached to a belt. Melanie's two friends each put on a belt and stand facing each other their arms out pretending to be trees.

Nothing happens for about ten seconds and then slowly the rope begins to turn, building up speed until finally it's going fast enough for Melanie to skip. And Melanie is a good skipper.

"Fire! Freezie! Disco! Fever! Sit! Split! Exit!"

JW looks up at the sky. Big dark clouds are rolling in from the ocean. Another half hour and Melanie's solar-powered skipping rope wouldn't have worked.

Melanie ends by doing a back flip through the turning rope. The crowd cheers loudly. Mr. Barber comes on stage and hands the microphone back to Melanie.

"My dad says I should say I'm looking for investors."

"Thank you, Melanie." Mr. Barber checks his program.

"Next up is Stephanie Marco. Stephanie."

Stephanie is in JW's English class. She comes on stage and takes the microphone while her younger brother Matt follows pushing what looks like a section of wall from a two-story house. Matt looks bored which is pretty much how Matt always looks. There is a window on the second floor and when Matt turns the wall around you can see that across the top of the window there is a brightly colored striped blind. A ladder leads to the upstairs platform and Stephanie climbs up to the second floor.

"Hi," says Stephanie. "I've invented a fire escape window shade for your child's upstairs bedroom." Melanie pulls the shade down to show everybody how pretty it is. "If there's a fire, this window shade becomes a way for your child to reach the ground safely."

"Fire," says Matt like the flames are four miles away and not to worry.

Stephanie stares down at him and frowns.

"FIRE!" yells Matt like the flames are licking at his sneakers. The crowd laughs. Matt grins.

Stephanie goes to the window and stands on the window ledge. Matt turns the display around so that Stephanie is now standing in the window facing the crowd. She has to be twelve feet above the stage. If this doesn't work, thinks JW, for sure she's going to hurt herself. Stephanie reaches up with both hands and grabs the wooden rod at the bottom of the blind which has half circle holes cut in it just for this purpose.

And with that she leaps out of the window. The crowd gasps. Then breaks into cheering as Stephanie floats down to the ground her window shade coming behind her like Superman's cape.

It is sometime before Mr. Barber feels he can interrupt the applause.

"My goodness, Stephanie. That was very impressive. Very. Can you do it again?"

Stephanie can and does.

Mr. Barber holds up his hands. "Our next inventor is Ty Randall."

JW looks on in surprise. Ty hasn't said anything about going into Inventors. Ty doesn't even like physics class except when it's over. Miguel follows Ty on stage. Ty is carrying a medium-sized black box and Miguel a big portable radio. They are both wearing white Crummie t-shirts streaked with red ketchup and yellow mustard.

"Hey," says Ty holding up the black box. "I've invented this wee goodie by accident at me buddy Miguel's stepmom's." Miguel makes a face and the crowd laughs. Ty brings the black box down to his chest and flips open the lid showing everybody there is nothing inside. Then he shows them the speakers built into the two ends and that the speakers are connected to the boom box that Miguel is holding.

"It cleans me clothes without using a washin' machine." That gets people chuckling. Ty puts the box down and opens the lid.

"You throw your dirty clothes into this box that has the speakers facing each other."

Ty takes off his dirty t-shirt and throws it in the box. Ty works out with weights and it shows. Ty gestures for Miguel to take off his t-shirt. Miguel does so but reluctantly. Miguel doesn't work out with weights and it shows. Ty makes a face at Miguel's jelly belly and the crowd howls. Ty holds up Miguel's t-shirt pointing out the ketchup and mustard.

"Sometimes those condiments at Crummie's can get away from you."

He pitches Miguel's t-shirt into the box and closes the lid.

"Then you put on Iron Maiden's *Hallowed Be Your Name* and turn up the volume as high as you can, like this..."

The volume of noise is impressive. So is Ty's dancing. This ought to help Ty's girlfriend rating, thinks JW smiling. Not that it needs any help.

"Make sure Miguel's stepmom's around... she hates this music... and when the song's over all the dirt in the clothes is lying on the bottom of the box. See?"

Ty opens the box and pulls out two sparkling white Crummie t-shirts which he and Miguel put on. The crowd is amazed. In fact everyone is buzzing with the possibilities. No water? No detergent? Do you think it would work with James Taylor? Just take longer, right?

When the applause dies down Ty holds the box upside down and out drop the two dirty t-shirts.

"Gotcha!" yells Ty.

"Thank you, Tyrone," Mr. Barber says. "We're always in danger of taking ourselves too seriously but with Tyrone around that just isn't possible.

"Let's see now, our next contestant is Jane Sommerville. Jane."

Jane looks about the twin's age. She's dressed like Alice in Wonderland in a blue dress, white stockings, white sleeves and a white apron. On the apron is a large clock face with arms that are turning in two different directions.

"Hi. I've invented a new way of measuring time. To start with I've gotten rid of seconds because no one wants to be second."

The crowd is enjoying this.

"From now on Seconds will be called MinUtes. Minutes will stay Minutes and Hours will be called Theirs because most of them seem to belong to someone else."

This gets a cheer.

"There will only be twelve hours in the day. This will get rid of the confusion between nine o'clock in the morning and nine o'clock at night. And everybody will only work four hours instead of eight."

More cheering.

"Lastly, I've gotten rid of February because it's such a depressing month, doesn't sound good and is hard to spell. Those 28 days I've added to July and August so that summer holidays will be longer."

With that the arms of the clock fly off, Jane curtsies and exits stage right.

"Thank you, Jane. My goodness those clouds look threatening. We'll have to keep things moving. Let's see. Our next student is Hanna Lee Chin from Granite High. What have you been up to Hanna?"

Hanna comes on stage wearing a large Mexican hat.

"Hi. I've always wanted something solar-powered that would charge my iPod when I'm outside. I started by putting solar cells on this sombrero but everybody laughed at me so that didn't seem like the way to go."

Hanna tosses her sombrero into the crowd. Now you can see the headphones. Hanna dances to the music she's hearing.

"So, I've invented a fiber-optics t-shirt that not only powers my iPod during the day," — Hanna shows the crowd the wire that runs from her iPod to the bottom of her t-shirt — "but at night you can reverse the flow and light up the t-shirt for safety."

It's dark enough now that people can see a faint glow from Hanna's t-shirt. It takes a moment for people to realize how clever this all is. Hanna walks off to sustained applause.

"Thank you, Hanna. That was very good."

There are only two more contestants to go. JW watches as Dougie leaves to go on stage. Gloria takes this opportunity to come over and stand beside JW.

"Hi, JW."

"Hi, Gloria. How are you?"

"Fine. Where's Niki?"

"Working."

JW looks at her daring her to say something about Niki. Gloria thinks better of it. "It was nice of your dad not to press charges against Douglas for going in your house."

They look at each other and despite everything JW laughs. Every kid in town has seen the cell phone video Eric took of Dougie jumping out the window into the hot tub.

"Are you going to do your bike thing?" asks Gloria.

"I guess so."

"Our next contestant is Douglas Brown who won last year's Inventors by recreating the Milky Way in a Coke Bottle. Douglas, what surprise have you got for us this year?"

Dougie tries to look modest.

"Well, I was working on the Douglas Brown No-Water Toilet but I couldn't get the bugs out — ha ha — get it? no-water toilet, can't get the bugs out? — ha ha — anyway, so instead of that I've come up with," — Dougie glances at JW and grins — "The Perfect Bicycle for Shipstead."

JW watches as Ernest "Don't Call Me Ernie" Brown comes on stage pushing Dougie's perfect bicycle. Ernie passes it to his brother, makes a face at JW and disappears.

"Here it is, The Perfect Bicycle. As you can see it has a large wheel at the back that the chain and pedals are attached to." Dougie points dramatically to this feature like a used car salesman trying to unload the biggest lemon on the lot. "And a small wheel upfront that I stole from my neighbor Mary Lou's tricycle." Dougie thinks people should laugh at this and they do when little Mary Lou, sitting on her dad's shoulders, yells out, "Douglas is weird!"

Douglas sticks his tongue out at Mary Lou and continues on. "Here's the ingenious part. This pipe running between the small wheel and the handlebars can telescope."

Dougie demonstrates this feature by sliding the handlebars up and down. "So, when you're going uphill the handlebars are down low and when you're going downhill they're up high, like this."

"Douglas, what about sideways?" Mr. Barber asks. "Most of us in Shipstead like to ride sideways." The crowd chuckles at this.

Dougie puts on his orange helmet, the one covered in mini-bumper stickers and climbs on his bike. He rides around the stage moving the handlebars up and down. While he's doing this Ernest comes back on stage pushing a very large wooden ramp. It's made of two pieces of plywood placed end to end so it's sixteen feet high and four feet wide.

Dougie picks up speed. "Here I go! The ramp is the same angle of incline as Harper Avenue! Here I go!"

Dougie's going as fast as Dougie can go when he hits the ramp. He pushes the handlebars down and now he's standing up peddling, pushing the bike from side to side. About two-thirds up Dougie's barely moving forward but he manages to turn the bike sideways. Just as The Perfect Bike for Shipstead is turning, getting ready to go downhill, Dougie pulls up hard on the handlebars.

Unfortunately for Douglas "Don't Call Me Dougie" Brown, last year's winner of Inventors, the handlebars never stop coming up and for one brief second Dougie's hands are high in the air holding the handlebars upside down three feet over his head. The look on Dougie's face moves from surprise to one of supreme disappointment. As his bike turns and begins to pick up speed it occurs to Dougie, as he rockets down the ramp, flies off the stage, waves one last time to Gloria, drops the handlebars and does a mid-air somersault, that his Moment of Glory will probably be, instead, a Moment of Gory. CRASH! CRUNCH! CRUMPLE! Dougie lies still.

"Do you think there'll be brain damage?" Gloria asks wrinkling her nose.

"How would we tell?"

"Oh dear," Mr. Barber says into the microphone. "Would someone call the ambulance please. Oh dear. And a storm coming too."

"Now JW, I'm sure Douglas would want us to carry on. You almost won last year with your perfect Christmas present, the Nike

Odor Eliminator Laces. What have you got for us this year?" Mr. Barber hands JW the microphone and smiles.

JW stands still looking out at the crowd. He's dumbstruck. The crowd waits thinking JW is up to something. Off to his right, Georgia and Paula are guarding Bicycle Booger.

The bicycle idea is gone. At least Dougie isn't going to win again. But then neither am I, thinks JW. He glances to his left. Sheriff Riley is standing in the front row gesturing to him. Sheriff Riley is using his finger to print letters on his chest. JW concentrates. F...B...I...

Now that he knows to look, there are definitely FBI-types strategically placed. A bunch of them. One is standing beside a big white cube van. Inside the van JW can see a woman in a white contamination suit. Then farther back he sees Ty and Miguel waving at him. He looks where they're pointing. There, on the knoll behind the crowd, is the Man in the Wheelchair, Max Keefer, better known as Rhino. JW scans the crowd for Max Keefer's bodyguards. He can't see them but they must be here too.

Booger, we've got danger here. Extreme Danger. Don't move. Don't do anything!

It's dark now, the sky almost black. There is a flash of lightning far out over the ocean. It's all so quiet.

JW watches as Sheriff Riley points at the black woman standing beside him. Special Agent Angela Burns. She's staring at JW. JW watches as she raises a walkie-talkie and begins talking into it. Then JW sees Max Keefer's two thugs pushing their way through the crowd.

Oh Boog, I never should have brought you here. I love you so much. I don't care about winning this, I just want to get you out of here where you'll be safe. I'm going to say something, make a joke or something, and then we're going to ride out of here. There'll be a lot of people after us so we'll have to be fast...

It's hard to describe the next three minutes without calling them the most famous three minutes in Shipstead's history. Certainly, for the people who witnessed them, these are three minutes of their lives they will never forget. Here's why.

On the stage, far left, there is suddenly a pinprick of bright light. Like a firefly. Then another and another. The crowd, which was getting restless, quiets now not understanding how these bright sparks are being generated. JW, standing on the other side of the stage, searches for his bicycle. It's not there but the twins are. They point at the fireflies. As usual Booger has taken matters into his own hands.

The little lights grow and divide, grow and divide. With each division there is a sizzle noise like a sparkler makes. The divisions pick up speed. Soon they are so fast the eye cannot follow them but the eye can see the multiplication. Where there was one now are a hundred fireflies, now a thousand, now ten thousand, now a hundred thousand, now a million, now ten million.

Now the fireflies are so close together they become one ever-evolving shape until at last there is a figure the crowd recognizes, primitive man. Hunched over, walking on all fours... Australopithecus, Homo erectus, Neanderthal, Cro-Magnon Man, Homo sapiens...

All of a sudden JW gets it. *It's Mick's evolution t-shirt come to life!*

Through the ages Man marches forward ever changing, ever growing, ever straightening, until at last Booger the Firefly Man stands facing JW. His skin shimmers and glows, ripples. He is plastic and sleek and still changing but now the changes are more subtle. A little taller, a little slimmer, forehead enlarging.

Booger you're fantastic!

Thank you, Mommy.

Booger turns to face the crowd. There is only the sound of the growing wind rustling the trees. A baby cries in the distance.

Booger changes from a man to a woman.

The crowd finally lets go. The cheer that erupts is like a clap of thunder.

But Booger is not finished.

He divides, the man emerges from the woman and stands beside her. Together they grow taller. Their heads change as their foreheads grow wider and higher. Booger is taking the crowd into the future now.

The man and woman turn and face each other. Fireflies of thought begin to travel back and forth between them like a cosmic tennis game. Then two babies form and they dance back and forth between their parents. Faster and faster the sizzling sparks fly until suddenly all four bodies explode upward into millions and millions of tiny lights. The Milky Way has descended on Granite Park.

For a brief instant the stars grow brighter and brighter.

Then there is a flash of lightning. Real lightning.

Thunder rumbles in from the bay.

The heavens open. In seconds everyone in Granite Park is drenched.

25

Two Weeks Later

"Then what happened?" Niki asks.

"I've told you all this before."

"I know. Tell me again."

Niki puts her head down on JW's shoulder. They're sitting on the beach in front of Crummie's, leaning back on the log, staring up at the full moon and a million stars. JW hasn't been right since Booger disappeared. Niki's hoping the beach and the ocean and talking about things will change how he feels.

"Booger evolved into these two incredible people, a man and a woman, future people, taller than us, with bigger brains. They sent thoughts back and forth between them like millions of sparks. Then they made two babies and then all the bodies became sparks, thoughts I guess, and then there was a flash of lightning and the sparks disappeared."

"They didn't need their bodies anymore."

"I guess."

JW knows Niki is trying to help him but his sadness is so deep he doesn't think it will ever go away.

"Then what happened?"

"It started to rain so hard everyone ran for cover."

"But who won Inventors?"

"Mr. Barber chose Stephanie Marco, the girl with the window shade fire escape."

"It's a good idea."

"Yeah, it's clever."

"But Mr. Barber said you would have won except who ever wins has to be able to demonstrate their invention at the State Science Fair and you said you couldn't do that."

JW is quiet after that.

"What do you think happened to Booger?"

"He hid in Jack Granite's flagpole."

"How do you know?"

"Booger told me." He also said *Goodbye Mommy* but JW hasn't told Niki that. He hasn't told anybody.

Niki gives JW a hug. "Booger's gone to the moon."

There are the beginnings of tears in JW's eyes now but Niki doesn't see them. JW rests his head on his arms. On the moon there is no food to eat, no water to drink, no air to breathe. Booger wouldn't have known that. JW should have stopped him. He should have grabbed Jack Granite's flagpole and run for it.

"I should have grabbed Booger and run away."

"The FBI would have stopped you, or that horrible Max person. Booger would be in a laboratory now."

"At least he wouldn't be dead."

"You don't know that."

"There's nothing on the moon."

Niki doesn't know what to say to this.

"What about the FBI?" Niki needs to keep JW talking. To make him see he's not to blame.

"Special Agent Burns came to Grove St. with Sheriff Riley."

"And?"

"Sheriff Riley said Special Agent Burns wanted to ask some questions."

"And?"

"She wanted to know where my Alien Being was."

"And?"

"I told her I didn't know and then I told her about Max Keefer stealing my bicycle and that he was at Inventors."

"And?"

"Special Agent Burns said she'd have a talk with him."

"And what did she say when you told her about Booger causing the accident by becoming the Monster from the Lost Lagoon?"

"She said 'Is everybody in California crazy but me?'"

JW can feel Niki's head shaking with silent laughter.

"Yummy says Jack Granite isn't going to bother her anymore."

"How does she know?" asks JW.

"He told her. Said he'd gotten involved with some bad people. Yummy's sure it's that Max person and his thugs. She says Jack Granite is selling everything including his mansion to pay them off. Jack Granite said Yummy was right, there are more important things in life than money."

JW tosses a stone at the ocean. "Speaking of Mr. Granite, he phoned me yesterday. Wants to know if I'd like to go to Astronauts' Camp next summer."

"Get out!"

Niki likes sitting beside JW. She likes how it's warm where he is.

"How do you like your mom's new house?" she asks.

"Mark Nash came for the weekend."

"No way!"

"He showed up in his limo. Mom told him to get lost. He came back in his Ferrari with a TV big enough to fill the wall. She told him she wasn't having any of that stuff in her house. Then Mark Nash says, 'What do you want?' 'A parrot,' says mom. So Mark Nash came back with a parrot."

"What did she name it?"

"Sheryl Crow."

"My dad phoned from Dallas. He wants us to move there."

JW's heart stops.

"And?"

"My mom told him we weren't moving ever again."

The only things moving at the moment are two hearts beating away and countless waves unraveling on the beach.

"How're your dad and Yummy doing?"

"I guess my mom's not too happy about them dating. She thinks that's the reason she and my dad aren't getting back together."

"That's hardly fair."

"They're going away this weekend without Amanda."

"That's great!"

"Did you hear Dougie has to pay back the thousand dollars he won last year?"

"No way!" Niki can't believe it.

"Yeah, someone showed Mr. Barber this European catalogue that was selling the Milky Way in a Coke Bottle for thirty Euros."

"I heard he got a phone bill for eight hundred dollars!"

"I wouldn't want to be just thoughts," Niki says.

"OMIGOD! JW!"

"What?"

"LOOK UP THERE!"

"Where?"

"THE MOON STUPID!"

JW looks up at the moon. There in the middle of the big bright circle is a word. A giant word. Then another and another and another.

HAVE

A

CRUMMIE

DAY!

"It's Booger! It's Booger!" Niki and JW are on their feet now jumping up and down, hugging each other.

"Way to go Booger! Way to go!"

Have A Crummie Day! flashes on and off several times and then disappears to be replaced by:

CLEAN UP

EARTH

OR

ELSE!

"Booger! You are so funny!"

JW cups his hands around his mouth.

"I LOVE YOU BOOGER! I LOVE YOU!"

The words on the moon fade and in their place come the words that will appear on the front page of every newspaper on planet Earth.

LaVergne, TN USA
31 March 2011
222237LV00004B/8/P